TARGET PRACTICE

"You going to move out of here?" the blond cowboy said. "Or we going to have to do it for you?"

"Let me tell you what's going to move," I said. "You're all going to move your hands up a little higher and un-buckle your gun belts and let them slide to the ground nice and easy."

"Boys, Sheriff wants us to drop our guns," the blond said to his three pals. "What you say about that?"

He started to draw when he came to "that," and I threw myself to the left off my horse, rolled over and came up on my knees with both guns out and shot the blond one as he was trying to move his gun to cover me. He lay there moaning with a hand covering his left shoulder, which had blood coming out of it. I was real upset. Here I'd gone for the middle of his chest and I'd got him in the shoulder. That had happened once before when I was younger, but I'd had two beers and wasn't feeling good. This time there was no excuse except I was out of practice. . . .

★ SHERRF ★
JORY

Milton Bass

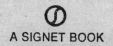

A SIGNET BOOK

NEW AMERICAN LIBRARY

NAL BOOKS ARE AVAILABLE AT QUANTITY DISCOUNTS WHEN USED
TO PROMOTE PRODUCTS OR SERVICES. FOR INFORMATION PLEASE
WRITE TO PREMIUM MARKETING DIVISION, NEW AMERICAN LIBRARY,
1633 BROADWAY, NEW YORK, NEW YORK 10019.

PUBLISHER'S NOTE

SIGNET TRADEMARK REG. U.S. PAT. OFF. AND FOREIGN COUNTRIES
REGISTERED TRADEMARK—MARCA REGISTRADA
HECHO EN CHICAGO, U.S.A.

SIGNET, SIGNET CLASSIC, MENTOR, ONYX, PLUME, MERIDIAN
and NAL BOOKS are published by NAL PENGUIN INC.,
1633 Broadway, New York, New York 10019

First Printing, June, 1987

1 2 3 4 5 6 7 8 9

PRINTED IN THE UNITED STATES OF AMERICA

For Michael and Lissa
who grew up along with Jory

★ 1 ★

You give a horse his head, and more often than not he'll take you home.

That's what must have been going on in some section of my own noggin because one part of me acted real surprised when I first came across landmarks I recognized, but the other part knew deep down that I was where I was because that's where I wanted to be.

When you got right down to it, it was more what I wanted it to be rather than what it really was. I'd never had what you'd call a real home, what with my ma dying when I could barely walk and my pa turning from Philadelphia lawyer to wandering drunk in less than five years. There were a couple of places and a few people that made me feel like I had a home—like with the Jordans when they took me in after my pa was booted to death by Ab Evans—but when I left there, I never had a wish to go back permanent. Sure, I'd like to see them again some day and get my pa's law books and maybe eat a few pieces of Mrs. Jordan's pie, but that wasn't where my horse or me had headed. We had come back to Mr. Barron's ranch that seemed to stretch from where the sun came up all the way over to where it went down again.

And I will have to admit that Amy Barron had never been too far in the back of my head in the two years I'd been away. Mr. Barron had wanted me to marry up with her after our showdown with the Germans when they nabbed the two of us while I was bodyguarding her, but I had never heard of nobody getting married at sixteen. She was old enough—twenty-one he had said at the time—but even though I might have looked the nineteen he thought I was, I wasn't thinking no nineteen. I was feeling very sixteen. So I had packed up my kit and skedaddled.

And here I was skedaddling back for reasons that I didn't quite know in my own mind. Maybe it had something to do with the fact that I had only eighty cents in my pocket and I knew that Mr. Barron would give me either a stake or a job. Maybe it was because of Amy. And just maybe it was because this was the only happy place I'd been in since my ma had died in Philadelphia.

I didn't relish the thought of coming back for a handout after I had rode out so grand two years before, what with everybody turning a little bit pale every time I strapped on my guns. Ever since I had come down to Texas, I had lived by the guns, which meant that other people had died by my guns. The Colts had been buried in the bottom of my saddlebag for almost eight months now, and I hadn't bothered once to oil or even unwrap them. Old habits die hard, though. Just the day before a rattler had spooked my big black and my hands had slapped leather and pulled way before my brain remembered that there wasn't no guns there in the first place. I kept twisting my mind to try to find something I could do that wouldn't need guns, but all I had ended up with was eighty cents. Nearly everybody I had ever met made his living without the need of guns, but I was one of God's, or maybe the devil's, exceptions. I knew I could always go back and help the Jordans with their store and livery stable, and probably that's why I never went back there. I couldn't twist my mind that much.

At first I thought I was in the wrong place because there were just too many houses for it to be Barronville. There were all kinds of side streets and people bustling about, and I could see a big, new church and what had to be a schoolhouse. I thought of that story my pa had read me about Rip Van Winkle, who had slept for twenty years and then come back to find everything so changed. But I'd been away for just two and it was like I had never been here before.

I didn't know nobody and nobody seemed to know me when I rode into the center of town, so I just let the horse pick his way until we came to a saloon that seemed to be called the Emily Morgan. That's what the sign said anyway. I figured her to be the owner. In my experience, Bill's Place was always owned by a man named Bill, unless he was dead and gone, or Cotter's Saloon was owned by a man named Cotter. Never thought about a woman owning a saloon, but I suppose there has to be a first for everything.

I am not a drinking man because of what happened to my pa. I have had a few beers, which I didn't like, and after the shoot-out with the Germans, I had drunk a whole bottle of whiskey because I was feeling so peculiar, but I didn't like the way it spun my head and roiled my belly, and I didn't ever want to go through that again. I've seen so much trouble caused by whiskey that it wouldn't surprise me if someday they did away with it. I don't know what a sober world would be like, but it would have to be better than what we got now.

It was pretty early in the day, but I could tell that some of the customers were already well on their way to what they figured was happiness when I stepped inside the doors and moved quick to the side like Jocko had said to do when he was teaching me the guns.

"Never stand out in the light when you come into the dark," he had said, and now it was as much a part of me as breathing. Everything that had to do with the guns was as natural as breathing to me, even if I hadn't even looked at them for the past eight months. Poor Jocko had bit off more than he could chew with that fellow named Jack that time I first came down the trail to Texas, and now he was buried out there in the middle of nowhere. But at least I had put his matched set of Peacemakers with the ivory

handles and the fancy holsters in with him before we
dropped the dirt down. I don't know about heaven or hell,
but it probably wouldn't hurt to have a pair of Colts in
either place. I loaded all the chambers and cocked the guns
before we threw the dirt on. Didn't want Jocko caught by
surprise two times in a row.

It was really dark in the saloon and I had to move slow
and easy before I got up to the bar so as not to stumble
over chairs or spittoons or maybe even a body. Sometimes
they don't sweep at night, and you find all kinds of things
the next day. I sure had enough experience in that kind of
thing with my pa near the end. One time I didn't find him
for two days, and it turned out he had crawled into a
wood box and didn't have the strength to pull himself out
again.

I was thirsty but I really felt foolish every time I had to
ask a bartender if he had a sarsaparilla or a root beer.
Sometimes they repeated what you asked in a loud voice,
and it was not always done with kindly intentions. One
time everybody in the bar started hooting and hollering and
yelling "Sarsaparilla" at one another, but that was when I
was still wearing iron, and when I stepped away from the
bar with my hands hanging extra loose, they shut right up.
Best of all, I would have liked some cool water, but they
didn't take it kindly if you didn't pay for whatever you
wanted, and you couldn't ask people to pay for a drink of
water.

So I moved up to the end of the bar where nobody was
standing and waited until the peaked-looking bartender
started to limp slowly down toward me. He recognized me
first but that was only because I couldn't have changed
that much and he was day and night to what he had been
two years before.

"Well," he said, and his smile showed he had lost
about five teeth in addition to whatever else was ailing
him, "look what the cat drug in and dumped on the
floor."

"Roy?" I said, my voice going up a mite because even

though I was sure who it was, I still wasn't sure it could be who it was.

"How you doin', Jory boy?" he asked, and stuck out his hand toward me. His grip was pretty good. Not as strong as it had been, but still pretty good.

"I'm doing fine," I told him, "but you look like you found a bronc that was tougher than you was."

"That's exactly what happened," he said. "Busted my leg, hurt my shoulder, knocked out my teeth and cost me my job."

"Hey," I said, "even if you'd lost your pecker, you'd still be the best foreman Mr. Barron could ever have."

"Barron's dead," said Roy. "Amy's married to a fella named Crutchfield, and he give me my walking papers. Or limping papers, might be more like it."

"Who killed Barron?" I asked, wanting to sort things out one at a time.

"He killed his own self. He was yelling at one of the hands over something silly and his face got all red and he just keeled over. Gone. I thought that man was going to live forever."

"And Miss Amy, how'd she get hitched to this new feller?"

"Army captain. Came to buy some beef and they hit it off, and when the old man went, she was kind of lost, and next thing you knowed they was married."

"And after you got hurt, he just let you go? Just like that? What did Miss Amy have to say about that?"

"She told me she was sorry, that she'd tried to talk him into giving me some other thing to do, but he wouldn't go for it. And he's running her and that place like he was still in the army. She tries to give me some money every time she comes to town, but I do all right here. Wouldn't take it even if I wasn't doing all right, but it so happens I am doing all right."

"How did you get to work in this saloon?"

"Work in it? I own it, boy."

"All you ever had was your saddle and your guns," I said. "How would you get a saloon?"

"I inherited it. Rich Englishman came to town and opened it up, and he hired me to help him because I knew the town and the people, and he up and died six months later and darned if he hadn't willed the place to me, lock, stock and barrels of beer. So I'm doing all right. How about you?"

He could tell by the slowness of my answer that even though I hadn't busted my leg, jammed my shoulder or knocked out some teeth, I didn't have no saloon going for me neither.

"Hell," he said, "if money is all it is, you ain't got no problem at all." He started to reach into his pocket.

"Hold on there," I said. "I admit I am a bit short right now, but I'm also short of taking any charity."

His face, which had paled out from the rawhide it had been, turned pink, especially in the cheeks.

"You've got some nerve to talk to me that way," he said in a voice loud enough to turn a few heads. "If you're too proud for charity, how about a loan? And if that's not good enough, how about becoming my partner and we split everything down the middle. Hell, you're as much family as I ever had, and you never know when some drunk is going to pick me off with his bad shooting."

"I apologize," I said, "and I will take the borrow of some money. But I don't want anything to do with a saloon. You know what booze did to my pa. I have other ways of making my living."

"Yeah," said Roy, peeking over the bar at my hips, "where are your guns?"

"I haven't had them out of my pack in eight months," I told him. "Just as soon leave them there."

"Ah," said Roy, "you used them some more after you left here."

I couldn't answer with words. Just nodded once. I thought back on how I had saved Mr. Kingman's life the year before, and how he had given me the job of foreman right out of the clear blue sky, and then I'd been pushed into a fight with the head wrangler and cut him down. What had stayed with me about that was I couldn't make it clear in my own mind whether I had killed him because he was the thief and coward I had called him out on, or whether it was because he was doing things in the church at night with Mr. Kingman's niece, one of the prettiest girls I had ever seen. Problem was she was as nasty as she was pretty.

"I been a foreman of a ranch," I told Roy, kind of proud maybe that I had been just like he was.

"You? What the hell do you know about being a foreman?"

"It ain't easy, is it?" I asked.

"Better than running a saloon," he said, and let the air right out of his lungs all the way down to the bottom. He pulled two bills out of his pocket.

"Here's ten dollars," he said. "Go get yourself cleaned up and buy what you need, and then come back here and we'll have some supper together and talk about the good old days and maybe even the days ahead."

"This is just a loan," I said. "I'll have this money back quicker than you can spit."

He just waved his hand at me and moved down the bar to where two fellers were banging their empty glasses on the wood.

I went outside and looked down the street for a place where I could get a bath and maybe a haircut and buy some clean long johns and a shirt and socks. The ones I had were pretty old friends and they smelled that way too.

Ten dollars. I had to make some money somehow so I could pay back Roy his ten dollars. I wasn't going to live on his charity or anybody else's. Had to make my own way.

There was a dry-goods store on the other side of the street, and I walked over to see what they had for what I needed. There were shirts in the window and other stuff, but that wasn't what caught my eye. Somebody had made a big poster and leaned it against some bolts of cloth. It had only two words on it, but I made up my mind the minute I read them. It said:

SHERRF WANTED.

★ 2 ★

The store was a mite larger than most of the ones I had ever been in, and was crowded with so much goods that you had to keep twisting your body this way and that as you cut your path toward the rear end. There was a short, chubby man behind the long counter who was paying out some change to an elderly lady who had a bolt of cloth under her arm. They both stopped and gave me a long look before they went back to their own business, so I just stopped and waited until they had bid each other good-bye and she had left after giving me one more long look. I had almost said "Howdy" to see whether that might poke a bit of friendliness into her face, but I was too tired, hot, and dirty to play social games. The man was looking at me. He wasn't going to say "Howdy" either. He didn't seem sure I was the kind of customer he wanted, so he let me make the first move.

"I'm looking for a new set of long johns," I told him, "and a shirt and a pair of socks. Then I need directions for the bathhouse in town."

He just stood there looking at me, and I couldn't understand why he wasn't moving or saying anything. Then it hit me, so I reached into my pocket and pulled out the ten dollars. They had barely cleared cloth but he was in motion, yanking out boxes and wrappers and running here and running there. God, money talks louder than guns sometimes.

It took a few minutes of holding different pieces up

against me to get the right fit, but we finally had it all down. He kept telling me what good material was in the stuff and how I was going to like everything to the point where I wished he hadn't broken out of his silence.

Just after he had handed me my change from the ten dollars and given me directions to the bathhouse, I popped the big question that had been in the back of my mind all the time we were having our fitting session.

"What about that sheriff-wanted sign in your window?" I asked him.

He stared at me for a second, then stepped back a space, and then stepped back another space. He wanted distance between us.

"Town's looking for a sheriff," he finally got out.

"What's the matter with the one you've got now?" I asked.

"He's dead. Somebody shot him in the back two weeks ago, and right now there ain't no official law in this town."

"Who shot him?"

I could see sweat pouring out of his face, and wondered what the devil was bothering him.

"Why do you want to know all that?" he asked, his voice quivering a little. He was suddenly twenty years older than he had been when I had walked into the store in the first place. What was he so scared about? I moved my hands through the air in front of me and then put them solid on my hips so he could see I wasn't packing any iron.

"I'm looking for a job," I told him.

"I didn't want them to put that sign in my window, but my wife made me do it," he said. Then he realized what I had told him.

"You're looking for a job? You're looking for a job as sheriff?"

"Could be."

"Are you a lawman? Who are you anyway?"

"Name is Jory," I told him, "and I worked at the Barron ranch a few years ago."

"The Barron ranch!" he almost yelled. "Why, they're the ones who . . ." And he shut his mouth like there was flies in the room.

"I been away for two years," I told him, "and I don't know much about the place now. Didn't even know Mr. Barron was dead until my friend Roy told me about it a little while ago."

"Roy? Roy over at the saloon?"

"That's the one."

"You're a friend of his?"

"Best one I ever had."

"And he said you should apply for the sheriff job?"

"No, that was my idea when I saw your sign."

"But you're not even wearing guns."

"All I have to do is strap them on."

"There's more to guns than strapping them on."

I don't know why I said it. Maybe because I felt I wasn't getting the respect that was due me, or maybe because trying to be a sheriff was a crazy idea, and maybe because I wanted the security of a job, any job, even one where the last one had been shot in the back.

"I can do more than strap them on," I told him, and I could see by his eyes that he understood that I meant shooting people if need be. I had almost used the word "kill" in my mind, so I had stopped short. I didn't want to think "kill." I was on the point of telling him to forget the whole thing and almost had my body half-turned to leave as I said it, but weighing down the other half of the scale was the four dollars in my pocket that was borrowed, knowing that I would never want to work in or even own a saloon, wanting no charity from anybody, using the only thing I was good at, and back there somewhere, way back there somewhere, wondering how Miss Amy would feel when she saw me wearing a badge.

"The town council is meeting tonight at the school-house," he said, and I could see the thoughts twirling in his head. "We start at half-past-six. Suppose you come over there at seven-thirty, and we'll have you talk to the whole bunch."

I didn't say another word, just nodded and left. It wasn't until I was soaking in the wooden tub that what I had done hit home to me. Did I miss the guns that much? Was this just a way of breaking them out of the pack again? What the hell did I know about sheriffing? Then again, I hadn't known nothing about helping to bring a trail herd of horses down to Texas, I hadn't known nothing about guns or breaking broncos or being a bodyguard or a foreman at the Kingman ranch and I had done all those things. Done some of them pretty good. And if I did get and did take the job of sheriff, I knew I was going to be able to do pretty good at that.

"Jory," I said to the bar of lye soap that was floating in front of me with the fat curling out of it into the water that my body had practically turned into mud, "you're eighteen years old and almost growed up."

★ 3 ★

Roy and I ate our supper in a little room at the back of the building. One of the bar girls served us the plates and then brought him a real beer and me a root beer. He must have told her beforehand because he didn't even ask me what I wanted to drink. You know, sometimes I think that the small things a friend does for you are just as important as the big ones. I ain't denying it's pretty vital to get help when someone's holding you by the throat, but when you think about it, that doesn't come up that many times in life. What's even better is when a person's figuring all the time on how he can make your life easier or happier. The bar girl gave me a smile as she set down my drink, and I smiled back at her as I marveled at how ugly she was with her pudgy face and crossed eyes. I ain't never but once seen a good-looking woman in a saloon. But I guess most *hombres* think that anything with two legs is better than ones with four.

The steak was as tough and stringy as a bronc'buster's ass, and the mashed potatoes had lumps in them as big as your knuckle bones, but after what I'd been forcing down my throat on the trail, even the chewing didn't seem like a chore. There was also a big plate of prime farting beans, some kind of pickled vegetables and a fresh-baked bread, and I didn't stop until there wasn't nothing left but scraps and crumbs.

"Gawdamighty," said Roy, "you eat more'n any three men I ever knowed and yet you're lean as a bean. How old are you now, Jory? Twenty-one? Twenty-two?"

"Thereabouts," I told him. It wasn't no real lie. Twenty-one ain't that far from eighteen.

"You got the face of a baby and the eyes of Methuselah," said Roy. "It's always hard for me to decide whether I had oughta spank you or ask your advice."

"I know you're a Methuselah," I said, "so I want some advice. I'm interested in that sheriff job."

His whole face wrinkled into one big frown and then he took a long drink of his beer before he slowly put the glass down again on the table. "You're probably the best there is with the guns," he said, "and you ain't afraid of nothing, but if you took on as sheriff, you'd be dead in a week."

"The man told me about the old sheriff. Said he was shot in the back."

"And the one before him was run out of town, and the one before that was beat up so bad that he can't see out of one eye and barely out the other. Sheriffs haven't lasted long in this place since Crutchfield took over the Barron place. The old man and me kept the hands in line while he was still alive, but now they can tear loose all they want. I even have a feeling Crutchfield prods them on. And that makes the hands from the other ranches and trail herds think that they've got to outdo them. Saturday night is kind of like a range war in this town, with people feared to go out on the streets."

"Can't nothing be done?"

"We're way the hell and gone from any real law. It's reached the point where the only way they're ever going to settle things down here is bring in the army and have them patrol the streets day and night."

"Sounds like you could use a sheriff."

"Oh, we could use one, all right. The way things are going we could probably use one every day. But I'd hate to have to bury you the first time you come back to see me."

"Hell, Roy, it can't be that bad."

"You're right. It ain't that bad. It's worse. But I can see

that you're going to try it no matter what, so you can count on my help come hell or high water.''

"They might not even give me the job," I said.

"Hell, they'll give it to whatever warm body has the guts or is crazy enough to pin on the badge. You've got both so you're a shoo-in.''

"Well," I said, pushing back my chair, "thanks for the feast. It sure was good to eat real cooking again.''

"You call this real cooking," he answered, "then you're crazier than I thought you was. Where you sleeping tonight?''

"Haven't thought about that.''

"Come back here and we'll put you up permanent or temporary, whichever suits your fancy.''

"I thank you," I said. "Now I've got to get my guns out and see if they still fit on my waist. Don't want to go to that meeting looking like a greenhorn.''

"Hell," Roy said, "if you walked in with a stick in one hand and a stone in the other, that would be good enough for them. And don't you take it on for less than a hundred dollars a month.''

The town seemed quiet enough as I walked toward the schoolhouse in the dim light from the glows coming out of people's windows. I didn't know what day it was because you lose track of things like that on the trail, but it sure couldn't be Saturday. Felt more like a Tuesday. I wondered if maybe Roy might be getting a bit skittish because the bronc busted him instead of vice versa.

There were five men, including the one who had sold me my itchy new shirt, sitting at a rough board table when I came through the door of the schoolhouse. They watched me without any smiles of welcome as I walked across the room to stand before their table. There weren't no ranchers or farmers among them because with the exception of one, they all had that soft look that goes with town living. I couldn't tell what they were thinking because town people seem to have two sets of faces and you have to peel off the outside one to see how they feel about anything. I try to be that way myself because it can save you from a lot of trouble, but I guess I ain't real town material to begin with.

"I'm Jory," I started right off, "and I'm here to inquire about the sheriff job."

"This is the one I was telling you about," said the man who had sold me the itchy new long johns.

They looked me over some more without saying anything. They didn't bother to tell me who they were, which was bad manners, but then again, I wasn't planning to marry any of their daughters, so it didn't matter that much. As a matter of fact, I was beginning to have third and maybe fourth thoughts about whether I wanted to work for this town or not. Maybe the best thing would be to borrow a stake from Roy and be on my way in the morning.

"Why do you want to be sheriff?" asked the only skinny one, who was dressed like he was going to either go to or arrange somebody's funeral.

"I'm looking for a job and I think this is one I can do," I told him.

"You know what's been going on in this town?" asked one of the chubby ones.

"I've heard tell."

"You had any experience with the law?"

"My pa was a lawyer and he taught me from his books."

"I don't mean that kind of law. I'm talking about keeping the peace."

"I've had experience in keeping the peace."

"He used to work at the Barron ranch watching over the daughter," said the one who had sold me the itchy new socks.

"Hey," said another one of the pudgy people, "I remember about you. You were in on the fight with the Germans. You're the one who's supposed to be so fast with the guns."

"I can take care of myself," I told him. This was taking longer than I expected, but at least the masks were starting to crack on their faces.

"Hell," he said, "if you're willing to try it, I'm more than willing to give you the chance. I'm for it. What about the rest of you?"

They all looked at each other for a few seconds and then they began nodding.

"Okay, it's settled," said the spokesman. "Job pays seventy-five dollars a month and you furnish your own bullets. You can have up to two deputies and they get forty dollars a month and furnish their own bullets."

"I'll take it for a hundred a month and I want three deputies at fifty dollars a month," I told them. Hell, I didn't know why I would want even one deputy, but if we were going to horse-trade, we were going to horse-trade. We finally ended up with me getting the hundred and two deputies at fifty dollars each.

"Your job is to keep peace in this town at all costs," said the man who had my clean body squirming in my clothes like there was fire ants all over me. "You come to my store tomorrow morning and I'll explain to you what kind of town we want and show you where the lockup is and where—"

"I want my hundred in advance," I told him.

"You'll get your money."

"I got to set myself up right if I'm going to do things right," I told him, "and for that I need money."

"How do we know you won't just take the money and skip off on us?" said another one of the pudgy ones.

"You people sure have a lot of faith in sheriffs," I said. "And in me. If you think you're hiring a thief, then maybe we just better forget the whole thing." I turned and headed for the door.

"Wait a minute. Wait a minute," two of them yelled at the same time. The thin one jumped out of his chair and came after me. I realized Roy was right. They needed me even more than I needed a job. From now on, the way to deal with them was tell rather than ask.

"We'll have your money in the morning when you go to Tom's store. You just don't pull a hundred dollars out of a hat. Now, what do you say you come back and let us swear you in?''

And that's what we did. I raised my right hand in the air and put the other one on a schoolbook because there didn't seem to be a bible in the place, which caused two of them to complain about the schoolmaster and what he might be teaching the kids. One of the pudgy ones spoke about preserving law and order and stuff like that, and I swore that's exactly what I would do. Then he pinned a really nice-looking badge on me that even had some weight to it so I could feel it pulling on my shirt, and they all shook hands with me, probably because they thought I didn't have long for this world, and I left them gabbing among themselves.

Business in Roy's saloon had picked up some when I got back, but it still had to be a Tuesday. Whether it was or not, it was Tuesday in my mind. People looked at me as I walked through the door, and I could see their eyes picking up the glint of the badge in the lantern light. Roy was serving people on the left-hand side of the bar, and one of his workers was serving people on the right-hand side. I walked over and stood in front of my friend.

''Well,'' he said, ''you went and done it. The root beer's on me.''

While he was slowly pouring it so it didn't all fizz over, a big fellow wearing two guns slung low, his eyes red from dust or maybe too much to drink, walked over and stood to the side of me.

''Well,'' he said in a voice loud enough to cause everybody's head to turn and stare in our direction, ''what have we got here? Looks like we might have a new sheriff. Finally going to get some law and order in this town. Better mind your manners, boys,'' he said, talking to the whole room, ''or you might get your wrists slapped.''

He got a few chuckles from a few of the men, but not enough to make him happy. Roy had just finished pouring the last of the root beer into the glass, set the bottle down and put his hands down behind the bar. I figured there was a sawed-off shotgun close by. The loudmouth wasn't pleased by the reaction from the crowd.

"What's that we got here?" he yelled, pointing at the root beer bubbling in the glass. "Hell, it looks like root beer." He picked it up and made a big deal about smelling it before banging it back down on the bar so hard that almost half of it splashed out, and this caused some more laughs. He was getting the crowd wrought up a little. "Damned if it ain't root beer," he cackled. "The sheriff drinks root beer. Hell, Sheriff, let me buy you a real drink."

"No," I said in a voice loud enough for everybody to hear, "I'm going to buy you a drink. I'm going to buy you a root beer."

"I ain't never drunk root beer," he hollered.

"Then you got a treat coming," I told him, and nodded to Roy, who quickly fetched another bottle and started to pour.

The prodder seemed a little confused by what had happened, and stood there watching, along with everybody else in the place, while the glass was filled. I picked up my half-glass and stood facing him, waiting for him to lift his.

"Nobody's going to make me drink root beer," he snarled at me like he was a coyote backed into a corner.

I put my glass down on the bar, moved one step back, and turned so that I was facing him full on. "I'm going to make you drink root beer," I told him, this time keeping my voice low and easy.

"What if I don't?" he asked, and there was a little bit of whine in his voice this time.

"Then maybe you ain't ever going to drink anything again," I said, and I let my hands drop to the pulling position. There was a bit of a quiver in my stomach because I hadn't touched those guns for eight months and I knew that the leather in the holsters had dried up and might stick. Right then I wasn't even positive I had loads in the chambers. I hadn't looked at the guns when I had pulled them out of the pack, just strung them on to show the town council I had them.

"What're you trying to do?" he asked, and there was real puzzlement in his voice.

"I'm trying to show everybody here that you're a loudmouth coward who would rather drink a root beer than die," I told him. "It's a choice you've got to make one way or another."

He didn't take long to think about it, but reached out his hand for the glass and started to gulp it down. But he was trying to drink too fast and it got caught in his throat, and he had to bend over and spit it out, gagging like he was going to throw up whatever supper he might have had. Crowds being what they are, they started to laugh, first one or two and then the whole place. A man came over and took the troublemaker by the arm and helped him across the room and out the door. I looked to see if he might have any other friends in the place who could be somewhat braver or drunker than he was, but nobody would look me in the eyes and they all went back to their funning.

"Well," said Roy, wiping up spills with a dirty rag, "that was some circus."

"Which one of us was the clown?" I asked him.

"I'm not sure about that yet," he answered, "but you're going to be a well-known sheriff by tomorrow morning."

"That good or bad?"

"Both," he said. "I'll say one thing, though: it sure felt good to see you in the saddle again. You ain't no boy no more, but I ain't sure what kind of man you've become. You just prodded one of Crutchfield's hands into almost getting himself killed."

"If I didn't do what I did," I told him, "I might just as well have laid that badge on the bar with the root beer."

"Might have been better-off in the long run."

"No," I said, "I'm not so sure. I think maybe, just maybe, I'm going to enjoy being a sheriff."

"Hell," said Roy, "get yourself to bed and do your dreaming there."

★ 4 ★

"If Nature is on your side," my pa always used to say, and the way he said "Nature" always made you think of it as having a capital letter, "then you don't have to worry about the human element." My pa taught me a lot in the five years we wandered together because we almost never had anybody else to talk to, and he said it was necessary for him to jabber away because if a lawyer didn't spout off all the time, his body could just blow up from the hot air inside him.

Nature was on my side when I woke up the next morning. Usually I fall asleep like somebody hit me with a poleax, but I stayed awake for maybe five whole minutes on the little cot in the room where we had taken our supper the night before, wondering about what I was going to do as a sheriff the next day, how I was going to act and meet people and maybe help them, or maybe have to put them in jail.

I'd seen plenty of sheriffs in most of the bigger towns I had been in, and they seemed to come in all shapes and sizes. Some of them just wandered the streets with a smile on their faces, saying hello to everybody, and some sat on a porch with the chair tipped back, not saying nothing to nobody, and some seemed quiet and some seemed noisy. The sheriffs didn't show up at the few saloon shootings I was witness to until everything was all over, and either the crowd was beating up on the lawbreaker or the shooter was already tearing out of town. Only once did I see a sheriff face down a man who had shot a gambler, and mostly that was because the cowboy was so upset about having killed somebody that he could barely keep his legs stiff.

What did a sheriff do all day? And how late did he have to stay up at night? Could he go to sleep before the saloons closed or did he have to wait until everybody else in town had gone to bed? The little room stunk of stale whiskey and beer and maybe some piss thrown in for good measure, and I didn't want to stay there another night. They had mentioned a jail, and maybe there was a place to sleep there.

There didn't seem to be nobody around in the saloon the next morning when I was all dressed up and my belly was crying for food, so I went out into the street by myself. This was where Nature was starting to help me because the sky was gray-black and there was a stiff breeze coming from the southwest, and it looked like it was going to pour buckets before the morning was out.

I headed right for the dry-goods store that was owned by the man they had called Tom the night before, and he was there moving stock around while waiting for his first customer, which was me because I needed a new slicker. Mine had just turned into yellow strips on the trail and wouldn't keep even a light dew from spilling through.

"Couldn't get all your money," was the first thing he said to me. "I've got sixty dollars and will have the rest by evening." He pulled a big wad out of his pocket and counted me out sixty dollars. Looked like he had at least another three hundred there, but that was probably his own and not town money. I wasn't going to push on it. It was fifty-nine dollars and twenty cents more than I had rode into town with the day before.

"Is there a place for me to sleep at the jail?" I asked him. "And where can I get my meals?"

"The jail just has the room for the prisoners," he said, "and a stove and a chair and a small table. Ain't no place there for anybody to bed down." He thought for a minute. "I hear," he said, "that Leona Davis has a room and is willing to feed whoever took it. She's had a tough time since Herb was shot.''

He could tell by my look that I needed to know more.

"Herb was the sheriff before you. Did a good job. Wasn't afraid of nobody and kept the peace as best you could in a town like this.''

"He the one shot in the back?" I asked, even though I knew the answer. "They know who did it?''

"If anybody knows, he ain't saying. It don't pay to draw attention to yourself around here.''

"This badge is sure going to draw attention," I told him.

"You asked to put it on," he said, and went to get my slicker.

He gave directions to Mrs. Davis' house, but all the time I was walking there I was wondering if it was a bad idea for the new sheriff to live at the house of the widow of the old sheriff. But the man had said she was having a tough time, and there was always the chance that I might be able to do something for her. I don't know why but I felt a kinship to her because her husband had been the sheriff until he was killed and I was the sheriff now. Kind of like we were relations.

The rain had started to come down a bit harder while I was in the dry-goods store, and I was wearing my new slicker, which creaked and groaned like a soul in torment. You had to break in those things just like you did a bronc or else you walked around like a wagon that had no grease in its wheels. There were quite a few people on the street by this time, but the slicker covered up my badge and they either just looked at me or didn't look at me, depending on how they were feeling. I was wondering whether I should be one of those "Howdy" sheriffs, but decided that could wait for another time.

The house was a little gray one on a side street with no other dwellings too near it. There were still trees and lots of cut brush just laying everywhere, so it must have been a new addition that hadn't sold all its lots yet. I knocked at the front door and took my hat off. It felt good to have the soft rain kissing on my face.

When the door opened, I got my first big surprise. Somehow, when anybody uses the word "widow," you think of somebody well along in years, maybe near forty, all dressed in black and with frown lines running down their faces. This was a pretty lady, a real pretty lady, and she couldn't have been more than twenty-five or so. And she wasn't in black, she was in brown, and there was something delicate about her look that made you feel the same way as when somebody hands you one of those pots they put flowers in and tells you it's a really costly one. She didn't say anything, just stood there waiting for me to explain myself.

"Mrs. Davis?" I asked even though I knew it had to be her.

She nodded but still didn't speak.

"My name is Jory," I told her, "and Tom at the dry-goods store said that you might have a room for rent and be able to provide meals."

"Please come in," she said, stepping aside for me to go through. There wasn't much furniture in the front room but it all looked clean and tidy. She motioned for me to sit in one of the two chairs, but somehow I couldn't do it and just stood looking at her.

"You're new in town?" she said.

It was my turn to nod.

"And how long are you going to be here?"

"I'm not certain of that, ma'am."

"What do you do?"

"I'm the new sheriff," I told her, and cursed myself as her hand went up to her mouth and tears started glinting in her eyes. Dumbest thing I ever did was to go there. What did I expect when her husband had been gunned down trying to do the job right? I vowed there and then I was going to find out who had done the shooting and bring him to law.

She pulled out of it quicker than a wink. She didn't try

to wipe away the tears, but her fist went down by her side
and became a hand again.

"Then you know about my situation," she said, and her
voice was steady and clear. God, I liked this kind of
woman.

"Yes, ma'am," I told her. "Mr. Tom said you needed
a boarder and I need to board, so if it wouldn't be too
much trouble, I'd like you to take me on. If you think it
would be too much trouble, I'll just go on my way."

"It's nine dollars a week," she said.

"I beg your pardon?"

"The room and three meals a day will cost you nine
dollars a week."

"That seems fair," I said, pulled out the money from
my pockets, and handed over eighteen dollars.

"One week in advance will be enough," she said.

'Ma'am, I have a favor to ask and I was hoping the
eighteen dollars would improve my chances."

"What's that?" she asked, her eyes narrowing a bit.

"I ain't had no breakfast yet today, and my stomach is
yapping at me like a coyote roundup."

She laughed. She laughed right out loud, took the eighteen dollars out of my hand and turned toward the back
room.

"Come on, Sheriff," she said. "Let's see what it takes
to fill you up."

There was a little boy sitting on a tall chair by the
kitchen table. He had a bowl of mush in front of him, and I
think as much was on his face as in his stomach. He didn't
say nothing, just held his spoon in front of him and stared
at me with his pair of round brown eyes.

"This is Todd," said Mrs. Davis. "Todd, this is Mr.
Jory. He's going to live with us for a while."

The boy cocked his head a bit and considered the proposition for a few seconds, then went back to eating his
mush. Little kids are like horses, you have to go at them
slow, so I didn't say nothing to him right then.

"I've got two eggs left," said Mrs. Davis, "and a loaf

of fresh-baked bread, and that's about all. I haven't had a chance to buy anything yet this week." I wished I'd given her more than the eighteen dollars, but I didn't want to try anything then and maybe hurt her pride.

"I may have to finish the loaf," I told her, "but that should keep me till lunchtime."

"Are you a hearty eater, Mr. Jory?" she asked as she rubbed a pan with a chunk of bacon and dropped the eggs out of their shells.

"I do get hungry, ma'am," I told her, "and if my board costs beyond human bounds, then we can make an adjustment in the rent."

"Let's see how it goes for a week," she said, sliding the eggs onto a plate and cutting some thick slices of bread to go with it. There didn't seem to be no butter handy, but the grease from the eggs was gravy enough for me. I set to and ended up eating three-quarters of the loaf before I realized this might be all she had for the day and I better leave some for her and the boy, who had finished his mush and gone off into the other room.

Mrs. Davis sat down in his chair and looked straight at me. "Where are you from?" she asked.

"I started life in Philadelphia," I told her, "but I been most every place since then."

"How come you're here now and took the job of sheriff?"

"I used to work at the Barron ranch two years ago," I said, "and I just sort of drifted back here without really knowing why."

The same look had come over her face that had come over that Tom fellow's face when I mentioned working at the Barron ranch, except that she didn't yell the way he had.

"I've spoke of that to two people in this town now," I said, "and both times they got funny looks on their faces."

"Nearly all the troubles my husband had in the three months he was sheriff of this town came from Barron people, and the night he was shot in the back he had a run in with Stark, the foreman."

I chewed slow on my last chunk of bread. Damn, it was good. Even as I was realizing that she was as much as saying that Stark was the one who had shot her husband, I was thinking how good that bread was and how I wanted to stay in town awhile and not go back on the trail to nowhere.

"I worked there when Mr. Barron was the boss and Roy was the foreman," I explained. "I don't know any of these new people."

She nodded, understanding what I was telling her.

"They never found out who did the shooting, did they?" I asked, just for something to say. A man gets shot down in the dark, there ain't much you can do about it.

"No, they never did," she answered, so low that I could barely make out the words. "But I think about it all the time. All the time."

"Maybe I can find out something," I said, once again just to fill in the silence between what she was saying and what she was thinking.

"You had much training as a lawman?" she asked.

"No," I admitted. "Only as far as the guns are concerned."

"Herbert had three years as a deputy over in Oaktown before he found out about this opening and came over to be his own boss, as he put it. He was a good sheriff, but he was never very good with the guns. As a matter of fact, he didn't like guns. Said they were a necessary evil. Do you believe they are a necessary evil?"

"I have found," I told her, "that they are necessary."

She stood up and took my plate away to the sink. "What time do you want your meals?" she asked.

"Whenever you eat, that's good enough for me," I told her, standing and stretching to ease up the strain from all those days on the trail. "I have to go see what the jail is like if you will give me the directions, and then I have to go see about hiring a deputy or two." I didn't know what I would do with them when I got them, but I figured somebody had to be around the jail when I was eating or busy some place else.

She turned around and faced me straight. "You're not going to get any deputies," she said. "There isn't anybody in this town who would take on those jobs. Herbert had to hire drifters who were coming through town and needed a stake, but as soon as they found out what it was like, they drifted right out again."

I wondered what she would think if she had known how close she had come to my own situation. I'd drifted in, and maybe after a day or two of this I would drift right out again . . . if I wasn't carried out.

"Well, I'm going to give it a try," I told her, "and then I'll be back to eat by noon."

"Don't you want to see your room?"

"Not right now, ma'am. I'm sure it's fine."

As I went out through the front room, I saw the little boy playing with a wagon that had been made out of whittled wood pieces. He stopped and looked up at me with those big eyes again. I almost spoke to him but decided that he wasn't ready yet. Nice-looking little boy, just like his mama. I wondered what his pa had looked like. Boy that age shouldn't be without a pa.

The rain was coming down real hard when I went out this time.

★ 5 ★

Mrs. Davis sure was right about those deputies. I found some old wanted posters in the office, wrote a sign on their backs, saying

DEPUTIES WANTED
SEE SHERIFF JORY
AT THE JAIL

and banged them up all over town, but nobody showed up the whole week.

This was where Nature came in again on my side. It rained so hard for five days that nobody was able to come to town from the outside, and nobody in town felt like stirring around much inside. The mud went up almost to the top of your boots in some places, and there was enough thunder and lightning so that anybody who had crazy cows to worry about sure had his hands full.

Word had gotten out about the new sheriff because people started nodding to me and some even said "Howdy." I howdied them right back because I decided I was going to be a smiling sheriff instead of one of those people who never cracked his face once. After all, I was working for the town and not them for me, so it was only right I be friendly.

The only occasion I had to be other than friendly was when a cowpoke who'd drifted in out of the rain from somewhere took himself drunk at a saloon called the Bull's Head and the owner, Tim Cahill, sent a boy running to

35

fetch me. The drunk was weaving around the saloon with his gun in his hand, but I could tell he wasn't in no shooting mood and I just went over and slipped it out of his fingers. Then I sat him down in a chair and unbuckled his belt, stuck the gun in the holster and told everybody to let the man sleep it off.

"He can pick up his gun at the jail in the morning," I said to Cahill. "No sense me dragging both of them over there in this rain."

He looked like he was going to give me a little argument about that, but decided to offer me a drink instead. Hell, that cowpoke was going to sleep all night with his body half across that table, and in the morning he'd be worrying more about what he was going to do to stop his head from hurting than causing anybody trouble.

My days got so orderly in the rain that I was almost disappointed when it decided to stop and let the sun peek through a bit. Mrs. Davis had finally allowed me to give her three dollars more a week, and she sure put out good grub for each and every meal. She told me she'd be in charge of neatening my bed each morning, and she also took care of my laundry for me. Her little boy got friendly enough so that we rolled a wooden ball at each other over the floor every once in a while, and more often than not there would be a pie or a cake on the table when I got back from my night rounds.

I visited my horse at the livery stable each morning, jawed a bit with Roy at his place in the afternoon and sometimes at night, swept out the jail every day, oiled up my guns and holsters and practiced the draw a little, though I didn't much feel like it. I wished I could be the sheriff without having to think of the guns as part of it, but that's what they were paying me for so I practiced till I got the motion and the timing back. I wanted to go out and shoot some cans around, but you couldn't do nothing in that rain. As soon as it cleared, I was going to take my big black for a run and get my shooting eye back, but I didn't feel no hurry with lightning cracking all over the place nearly every day.

On the morning the sun was trying to work its way through all those black clouds, I came to the jail about eight o'clock, and there was this tall, thin cowpoke leaning against the wall. At least I thought it was a tall, thin cowpoke until I came up on her. That's what I said—*her*! Danged if it wasn't a woman, of the female sex. She was dressed just like a man, and she was holding one of those English "greener" scatterguns with a sawed-off barrel. It was like coming across one of those freaks of nature, like a two-headed calf or a bull with his horns all intertwined among each other.

"You're Sheriff Jory," she told me, and I nodded to show her that I knew who I was.

"I'm Andy Colvin," she said, and stuck out her hand at me. It took me a few seconds to realize that she wanted to shake, so that's just what I did. Her palm was all sweaty, which made me look closer at her, and I could tell that this lady was close to trembling in her boots. Somebody had scared the hell out of her and she had come to the sheriff for help.

I pulled the key out of my pocket, unlocked the door and motioned her inside. I saw her shiver as we went in the door, but the room was so cold and musty before I got the stove going each day that I always did a little bit of a shake myself.

"What can I do for you?" I asked once we were inside. I left the door open so nobody would think there was anything peculiar going on.

She took a deep breath, opened her mouth, let out the air, and took another swallow in. "I'm here to apply for the deputy job," she said, and it was my turn to let the air in and out of my body a few times. Here I was all alone in a room with a crazy woman who was carrying a shotgun and who could tell what she might come up with next.

"That's a job for a man," I told her. "Ain't no woman ever been a deputy."

"There any law that says a woman can't be a deputy?" she asked, and I could tell from the way she asked it that she knew she was on thin ice and that was what was making her so nervous. I busied myself putting kindling in the stove and lighting it up, but even by the time I got through dallying with that I had no answer. There had to be a law somewhere about that. You couldn't expect no woman to go wading into a bunch of drunken cowpokes in a bar, or stop a bad man from shooting somebody else, or face down anybody who refused to keep the peace.

"There's the law of common sense," I finally came up with. It wasn't much but it was the best I had at the moment. Gawdamighty, this was the last thing I thought I'd have to go through when I took on the job of sheriff.

"I'm as strong as most men," she said, "and I can outshoot any man with the 'greener' or my Sharps."

"How about with a six-gun?" I asked, desperate to find reasons to get her the hell and gone.

"Ain't never shot a six-gun," she admitted. "But they ain't worth a hoot at no distance anyway."

There was truth to what she was saying as far as the average six-gun wearer was concerned, but I wasn't going to get in no debate with her about shooting or brag about what I could do. Besides, it was one thing to wear a pair of guns on your waist where hardly nobody noticed them, and another to go around lugging a shotgun or a rifle. You didn't do that even on the range. How was I going to get this girl out of my office and out of my life?

"Keeping law and order can be a risky business," I told her. "You have to spend a lot of your time in saloons that are full of drunks or people on the prod or gamblers and thieves and . . ." I wasn't quite sure what you would call the saloon girls to a proper woman, if that's what this one really was. I'd heard them spoke of as most anything, but I wasn't going to say even one of the not-so-bad words to this girl. "All sorts of other people," I finally came up with, "and the men would be 'shamed if they was told to do something by a girl and the women there would be spitting mad at you and even using swear words."

"Is that all there is to the job?" she asked. "Is that the only thing you do?"

She was getting my back up and I could feel the red pushing into my face.

"No, that's not all I do," I told her. "I have to patrol the town and check the doorways of the stores, and tell husbands not to beat on their wives, and see that drunks get home and don't sleep on the street and tell people to keep their dogs from biting other people. You can't imagine what a problem there is with dogs. Everybody thinks his dog is perfect and everybody else's dog is a varmint. So far, I've had more trouble with dogs than anything else in this town."

"There you are," she almost yelled, and she sounded like she had just laid down a royal flush for the big pot of the evening.

"There you are what?" I asked her.

"I could be the deputy that helps with the patrolling and the dealing with the families and some of the drunks if they ain't too heavy and all of the dogs. How would you like it if you never had to deal with no dogs ever again? A woman could do all that. I know damn well that this woman could do that."

I usually get embarrassed when a woman uses a swear word in front of me, but from this particular one it almost seemed natural. There was something about her that I liked despite all the trouble she was giving me. She was a tall one, that was for sure, with broad shoulders and arms that looked like they'd carried some firewood from way over somewhere to right over here. She was kind of built like some fence wire with none of the usual woman things sticking out of her, but she had a nice face even if it wasn't a very pretty one.

"Where you from?" I asked her, hoping to get off the main topic for a bit until I collected my wits some more.

"My pa had a little spread over to the west of here," she said, pointing her shotgun in that direction. You could tell it was a gun that had been used plenty, but it was also one that had been well cared for. "There's a good spring there and we run a few head of cattle and some barn animals and we was almost getting by."

She stopped and looked at the wall for a minute, and I wondered what had come over her.

"Three weeks ago," she went on, "I found him in the brush about a mile from the place. He'd been trampled to death."

"Your cows run over him?" I inquired as she stopped and looked at the wall again.

"We didn't have that many cows," she said, "and I would swear there was iron behind some of the marks on him. The cows had disappeared and I ain't found them since."

"You think some rustlers done in your daddy?" I asked.

"Ain't no way of knowing," she said. "You see, my pa was a drunk, and no matter what I come up with, everybody would say he fell off his horse and was kicked to death by his own animal."

"My pa was a drunk, too," I told her, I don't know why. But it was a kinship with each other that had nothing to do with blood but everything to do with life. I wished I could give her some money or help her out some other way, but there was no way she could be a deputy. "You still living out at your place?"

"For now," she said. "Crutchfield came by two days ago in the rain and said he was sorry to hear about my daddy, and maybe he could buy up our spread and give me a little money to make a new start someplace. Which was mighty strange."

"Why?"

"Because I hadn't told nobody about my pa being dead. I had buried him in the field behind our cabin, but I hadn't had no time to put a marker or anything on his grave. You wouldn't even know where it was in the tall grass."

Crutchfield. Amy Barron's husband. The one who had fired Roy because he'd got his body busted doing his rightful job. A man who knew somebody was dead that nobody knew was dead. A man who might want a little place because it had a good spring. I'll have to admit that none of this would have gone through my mind if he hadn't been married to Miss Amy, but there were a lot of things that didn't ring right when his bell was struck. This poor girl could have been one of them.

"I sure sympathize with your predicament," I told her, "but being a deputy is just out of the question. First of all, I don't think the council would put up with it."

"You the sheriff or ain't you?" she asked.

She had me there. If by some crazy chance I would have wanted her for a deputy, wouldn't have been nobody told me I couldn't. But I might have enough to worry about without being nursemaid to a girl on top of it. I decided to make believe I hadn't heard her question.

"There must be other jobs for you to make a living at," I told her. "Why, just the other day I heard Tom at the dry-goods store saying business had become so good that he was thinking of hiring a clerk. You could—"

"I'm a ranch girl," she said, sticking her pointy chin straight at me. "I was born on a ranch and I ain't never going inside for nobody. I shot all the meat for me and my pa, I split all the wood, I carried all the water, I helped with the branding and the gelding, I've broke broncs and I ain't afraid of nobody. I'd rather die than work as a clerk in a store."

"I know how you feel about those things," I told her, even though I was finding town life not such a hard way to go. But what I wanted was to get her out of the office as easy as I could and send her on her way. "My pa always used to say that something will always turn up when you need it." That didn't work out very often, maybe never, for my pa, but I wasn't in the business right then of giving this girl more discouraging news than she already had. I wondered about offering her some money to tide her over, but there was so much spunk showing that I figured she'd be more mad than grateful.

"Look," she said, "I ain't had hardly any schooling, I

don't even have a dress and I'm a terrible cook. When you get right down to it, I'm more man than woman. I can handle the deputy job. Just give me a chance so I can show you.''

Things had gone far enough. There was no chance to wheedling her out of the place, so I would just have to close it out cold and clear.

"Miss Andy," I said, "there ain't no way I can hire you for the job. Now I have to go about my duties, so I can't give you no more time." I took the plunge. "If a little money would help, I'd be glad—" Her look shut my mouth like a mouse had gone for the cheese.

"You keep your old money," she said. "I still got enough shells to get me meat and I can take care of myself. And you'll be sorry you did this because someday I'm going to show you how wrong you were."

She was out of the place quick as a cat. I liked the way she moved. I went to the door but she was no place to be seen. I wished I could disappear like a mountain cat sometimes. One second you're there and the next you're gone.

Crutchfield. The things kept piling up where that man was concerned. I wondered if I was ever going to meet him. And Miss Amy. I knew I was going to meet up with her one way or another. If it wasn't in the cards, I was going to call for a new deal.

★ 6 ★

It was Todd's fourth birthday, and Mrs. Davis put on a
spread for supper that looked like it would keep us going
until his fifth one came around. She hadn't told me nothing
about it, so I didn't even have a present for him, but I
went to my poke in the bureau and pulled out two silver
dollars that I clunked into his little hand. Mrs. Davis got
all flustered and said I hadn't ought to do that, but Todd
was having such a good time banging the two coins together that she couldn't help but laugh and we got by it.

The only good food I had ever eaten was when I was
working the livery stable for Mr. and Mrs. Jordan and
living with them at their house after my pa was done in,
but I must say that Mrs. Davis set as fine a table as Mrs.
Jordan even though she was heaps younger. A man's got
to be real lucky to come across food like this *twice* in his
lifetime. There was a good-sized roasted chicken and stuff-
ing like I'd never tasted before and a mountain of mashed
potatoes and gravy to swim in it and beans and bread and
pickles and relish and a chocolate cake that seemed a mile
high.

We usually didn't talk much at meals, but Mrs. Davis
was in high spirits because of Todd's birthday, and she
kept smiling at him and sometimes me and chattering away
to both of us and telling how she'd had a letter from her
husband's folks in Ohio and they'd sent her some money
and told her to come live with them on their farm.

"You going to go?" I asked her, thinking of myself

mostly and where I was ever going to find another place to eat and sleep as nice as this one.

"I haven't made up my mind," she said. "With you as a boarder, I'm getting by very nicely and I like Texas better than I liked Ohio, and if we go back to the farm, I'm going to end my days as the widow of the family's oldest son."

"You certainly have your perplexities to deal with," I told her.

She looked at me like she was going to speak, changed her mind, and put some mashed potatoes in her mouth, then changed her mind again and asked her question.

"Jory," she said, "may I ask you a question?"

By that time I had forkfuls of chicken, potatoes and beans in my mouth, so I could only nod and chew.

"How much education have you had?"

"Schooling?" I asked her. This time she nodded, but without the chewing. "Ain't really had much formal schooling," I told her. "When my pa and me left Philadelphia, we drifted around quite a bit before we ended up in Kansas. Once in a while we would stay in a place for a while, like when we were in Saint Louis, and he'd bring me over to the school, but the longest I ever stayed in one was two months. I've always been big for my age, and sometimes they would stick me in with the little kids because I didn't have no mathematics to speak of and other things like that. Then the bigger kids would get funning at me, and I wasn't as happy as I could have been. Mostly what I learned in school was how to fight people who were funning me. How much schooling did you have?"

"Quite a bit," she said. "As a matter of fact, I was a teacher for nearly two years before I was married. You don't mind me asking about this, do you?"

"No, ma'am," I told her. "Figured you must have a reason."

"Well, something's been bothering me. Most of the time your words indicate that you haven't had much schooling, but quite often you come out with a word that stops me dumb in my tracks. For instance, you said 'perplexities' when you were talking about my situation, and that's not a word that's used very often in most places and not at all around here. And you keep using legal terms to describe situations, words that I vaguely know but would never think of using.''

"That's simple to explain, ma'am," I told her. "Wherever we went, we always dragged my pa's law books with us, and almost every night after he taught me how to read, we would sit for a spell over the books and he would explain what everything meant as best as I could understand it. And then he would have me reading from the books until he went out to the saloon or fell asleep and then I could stop. But sometimes I got interested and kept going over things by myself. My pa was a drunk and people shunned him, and I never had no kids to play with, so there was just the two of us and the law books, and some of those words have rubbed off on me.''

"I'd be happy to help you with any schooling you would like to learn," she said.

"There are two things I always thought I would like to know more of," I said. "Numbers and history. Every time I have to work with numbers I get into a terrible sweat. And from what my pa told me about the Greeks and the Romans and people like that, I know I'd like to study up on where we came from and how we got where we are right now.''

"Sheriff?"

"What?"

"You want history to explain to you how you got to be sheriff of Barronville, Texas?''

I could tell from the little smile on her face that she was funning me a bit, and Todd banged his dollars together, and I thought how nice it would be if Mrs. Davis wasn't so old. Gawd! I realized that I was thinking marriage thoughts, and I helped myself to a third piece of the cake.

It must have been that third piece that done it because after supper I just felt like I wanted to lay down on my bed and sleep for a while. I usually made the rounds right after I ate and maybe jawed with Roy awhile and was back in the house by near nine and asleep right after that. I was wondering what would happen if I let one time go by without doing my duty. It was rare that I bumped into any of the town council on the street after dark, so they wouldn't know I had let things slide a little. I met the problem halfway by falling asleep in the one soft chair in the parlor, and must have been gone a good half-hour because when I opened my eyes, Mrs. Davis had the kitchen all cleaned up and was sitting and knitting in the hard chair on the other side of the room.

"Glory be," I told her. "You didn't put none of that stuff the Chinese smoke into the food, did you?"

"If I had," she said, laughing, "with the amount you put down you would be dead rather than asleep."

"Time to do my chores," I said, standing up and stretching and reaching for my guns on the table.

"Why don't you take a night off?" she asked. "Looks like it may start raining again, and it sounds pretty quiet out there. Nobody will notice if you miss one night."

"Yes, they would," I told her. "I'd notice."

She put her knitting down on her lap and looked at me with a frown on her face. "You know," she said, "sometimes you're so like Herbert that it scares me. I don't know how many times I asked him not to go out again, and he would just smile and buckle on his guns and go do his job. And while I was sitting here or lying in bed waiting for him, I would strain my ears as hard as I could to pick up the sound of any gunfire. It wasn't until he was back safe in the house that I could relax again. And even then, I knew that on the next night he would be going out again. If you stay a sheriff, Jory, never get married. You'll save some woman an unhappy life."

She caught me by surprise with that.

"Weren't you happy?" I asked her, and I guess I caught her by surprise, too, because she took an extra second before she answered.

"Yes," she said, "I was happy. Even if I'd known what was going to happen just as I know now what did happen, I was happy."

I could see tears in her eyes as she got up and went into the kitchen. I had to learn to keep my mouth shut. Here I'd went and spoiled Todd's birthday for Mrs. Davis with my waggling tongue. I thought of going into the kitchen and saying something, but I knew I would only make it worse, so I put on my hat and went out the door.

It was a dark night with a bit of a chill in it from the black clouds that were moving back to us from wherever they had gone for a spell. I hadn't thought it was that cold out, so I didn't have my canvas jacket on, but this was going to be a quick tour and I figured I'd warm my blood up by moving fast.

Nature, as my pa used to say, don't always work the way you either plan on or hope for. "What about God?" I had asked him once. "He's the most unpredictable of all," he told me, so since then I've always depended on myself to keep things straight. If Nature makes it cold, I put on some covers if I can; if someone points a gun at me, I don't stop to pray.

Things looked regular as I walked down the street, shaking the door of the dry-goods store to see if Mr. Tom had remembered to lock it, howdying the few people who were still on the street and feeling better with walking that supper off. I didn't plan to go in any of the saloons, even Roy's, because I didn't feel much like talking to anybody, but Nature or maybe even God took a hand in there somewhere. Because just as I was halfway down Center Street, two shots boomed out from the Paris France Saloon, which was maybe two hundred feet away.

This was the biggest and fanciest dance hall and gambling palace in town, maybe twice the size of Roy's place. The owner, Fred Murchison, was one of those loud people in both dress and manner. He was always smoking a big cigar and slapping people on the back and laughing out loud over things that weren't really very funny. He would offer me free drinks every time I went into the place, and once even tried to give me ten dollars after I told a man who had busted a chair on the floor to get out of town before I made his ass sore.

I always walked through the Paris France just like I did every other saloon in town, but I didn't at all like the place. It had two floors with a balcony all around the top, and there were little rooms where the girls would take the men upstairs, and there were big mirrors on the walls and two paintings of naked women laying down on couches and pink shades on the lamps, and the females all wore fancy dresses with things hanging off the bottoms. A few of them looked pretty good from a distance, but they all smelled of sweat when you got real close even though they doused themselves in toilet water all the time. This was nothing against them because everybody usually smelled of sweat except for Mrs. Davis and a few others, including me when I could get to the bathhouse every week, but the Paris France was not one of my favorite places to visit.

There usually was no problems there because Murchison had two big bartenders who'd as soon pound a man on the head as serve him a drink, and it was just by chance that I was in the place when the fool broke the chair. He was lucky I reached him before the bartenders did because his whole body would have been sore by the time they got through with him.

I didn't run because I have learned it is not a good idea to try to handle trouble while you're breathing too hard, so by the time I reached the stairs two more shots had went off. When I came through the doors and stepped to the side, I was so surprised at what I saw that even Todd Davis could have come up and taken my guns away before I could have done anything about it. In the middle of the floor was one of Murchison's calico queens with her dress tore all the way down to her waist and her two big dugs hanging down like those of a cow in pain way past her regular milking time. Standing near her was this big galoot with his gun half-raised in the air, so he had to be the one who had done the shooting, and in back of them were five or six cowpokes laughing and hooting and enjoying themselves like they were at some kind of banjo show.

As I stood there for the few seconds it took me to realize what was going on, the big man weaved enough to show he was drunker than a coot, and then he yelled, "Don't ever tell me where I can put my hands. I put my hands any damn place I please. And now I've got a good mind to make you show everybody what the rest of you looks like, you dirty cow."

Everybody but the men who were whooping and hollering had been sitting still and quiet, hoping they could get out of there without being hurt, but when the gunman yelled out what he did, even his own friends stopped their noise. I don't know whether it was because they thought this was going too far or because they were thinking what it would be like to have a naked woman standing there in front of them in the middle of a whole saloon.

Whatever it was, it was also time to put a stop to it, and I stepped toward the middle of the room and called out, "That's enough of all this. You stop right there and let this girl go get her dress fixed up." It maybe wasn't what had to ought of been said, but those were the words that come out of my mouth. I was feeling more 'shamed for the poor woman than for anything else, so I guess I wasn't thinking too straight about what I had walked into.

The drunk turned to look at me, the gun still half-raised in the air. "What the hell we got here?" he asked himself as well as everybody else in the room. He seemed like a man who wasn't used to being interrupted in what he was doing. "Goddamn," he yelled, "it's the new sheriff. Hey, boys, we're finally going to meet the new sheriff."

"Put your gun away," I told him, speaking soft and easy so he could hear only if he strained his ears a bit. It puts people off just enough sometimes when you make them go out of their natural position. Right then he was thinking more of catching what I was saying than he was of the gun in his hand. "Leave the girl alone and put your gun away."

"My gun's out and ready," he said, "and yours are stuck in your pants. Maybe you should join the party, Sheriff. How would it be if you was to take your clothes off and stand beside the lady here? How would that be, Sheriff?"

"You drop the muzzle of that gun one inch," I told him, "and my guns are going to be out of my pants, and you ain't ever going to tear anybody's clothes off ever again."

He stopped and thought about that a second or two, carefully not moving that gun the one inch I had told him about, and I thought maybe we were going to get home free. But then I could see an idea cross his mind. For a second I thought his eyes might light up with what was going on inside his head, and I watched them carefully to see if he was about to make his move. But he had different plans.

"Boys," he said, "I want all of you to spread out a little so that the sheriff can see how many friends I've got here." The men behind him looked at each other, and they caught onto the idea inside this gunman's mind. They spread out about two paces apart and dropped their hands down in the pulling position. Three more of them came out of the tables somewhere and joined the bunch. Which made nine of them. I was being told that if I drew my guns, ten people would be shooting at me. Maybe I'd get one or two, but sure as shooting I'd be full of bullet holes from the rest of them.

"Now, Sheriff," said the boss man, "we don't want no more trouble here, so I'm just going to walk over to you and take your guns and then maybe we'll have a drink or two together before we go back to the ranch."

There wasn't no chance of me giving up my guns to this crew. If I did, I'd either be dead or they'd beat me into sawdust or they just might make me take my clothes off and stand beside the poor girl in the middle of the floor. If shooting started, she was right in the line of fire, but she was too scared to move. The gunman took one step toward me and then stopped when he looked at my face. He knew that if he took one more, I was going to draw and his men would probably kill me but there was just the chance that I might get him first. With my guns still in the holster, there was only a slim chance of that happening, but that was enough to make him think about taking that next step.

I don't know who won the debate inside him, but I have the feeling he was going to take that step or maybe shoot at me first and then take the step, but just before his gun came down that one inch, a boom ripped through the building that made your ears ring, and a big hole was blown in the floor right between the toes of the boots of the gunman. Like everybody else, I had no idea in hell what had happened, but I recovered quick enough to get my guns out and ready to roll.

"There's another load in the other barrel," a female voice called out from somewhere in the balcony to the left of me, "only this one's loaded with nailheads. Anybody makes a move, the whole bunch of you are going to be chewing nails."

Gawdamighty, I knew who it was. It was that crazy Andy Colvin who'd been pestering me that morning. I looked down at the hole in the floor between the gunman's feet. She said she could shoot, but I didn't think anybody could do that with a shotgun. She had to make her own shells and know exactly what she could do with each one of them. Half the people in the place were looking at the hole the way I was, and the other half was staring up into the balcony to see if they could make out who it was in the gloom up there. The friends of the gunman were too surprised to have drawn and had no desire to meet up with nailheads, so me and the gunman were the only ones with weapons out. I holstered my left gun, walked up to him, and stuck the right one into one of the holes in his nose. I don't know why I did a crazy thing like that. Except that a few seconds before I knew I was a dead man, and now I knew I was going to live. And since I was going to live, this son of a bitch was going to pay through the nose for my discomfort. Literally, as my pa used to say. I wondered if Mrs. Davis would think that a fancy word.

As I took the gun out of his hand and stuck it in my waist, I noticed something peculiar. Damned if the man hadn't soiled himself, as I once heard Mrs. Jordan say when she was taking care of a neighbor lady who had some bad disease. He stunk like a cow barn in August. I looked behind him at his friends, and they all had their guns in their holsters and their eyes still glued to that balcony.

"Listen, you people," I called out to them, "I want all of you to unbuckle your gun belts real easy and lower them real slow to the floor."

Nobody tried to debate the proposition. A couple of them started before I even got to the last word, and then the rest of them followed suit. There might have been a couple there who because of drink or pride would challenge what I'd told them to do, but they could all see the hole in the floor and they were all thinking what their bodies would look like if a fistful of nailheads went through their faces.

All of a sudden I realized that the poor, shaking, half-naked girl was still standing like she'd been rooted to the floor, tears running down her face and hands clutched so tight together that you could make out each bone like it was on a skeleton.

"You go get yourself fixed up, miss," I told her and she broke and ran to the side, where two of the other girls grabbed her and hustled her off somewhere.

"Now," I said to all the troublemakers, "this here party is over for the night. I don't know where you're from, but wherever it is I want you to go back there. If you're from a trail herd, you can come get your guns at the jail tomorrow and then I want you out of town. If you're from around here, you can come get your guns tomorrow and we'll talk about if and when you can come to town again."

I took my gun away from the nose of the troublemaker and he sagged like he was going to fall down.

"As for you," I told him, "this town is off limits until someone gives me a good reason why it shouldn't be. And it better be a damn good reason. Now get out of here, all of you, and I mean fast."

They had barely reached the door when old Roy came busting through on his gimpy leg with a shotgun in his hand and a wild look on his face. He used his gun to shove aside the men who were coming at him, and didn't slow down until he caught sight of me standing in the middle of the floor.

"They told me you were in trouble over here," he said.

"That's a good way of describing it," I told him, "but the trouble's all over for now."

I turned toward Murchison, who had been by the bar while all this was going on and hadn't moved a speck the whole time. You'd think a man would do something when one of his workers, especially a woman, was being done wrong by a pack of mad dogs.

"You get me a gunnysack," I told him, "and have all those guns put in it."

He motioned to one of the bartenders and the man moved fast.

"Andy," I called out, "you can come down now."

Everybody watched her while she was coming down those stairs, just like she was a queen or something, or maybe because they figured her as a freak of nature. When the men had dropped their guns on the floor, I had heard the quick click as she had broken the barrel of her gun and put a new shell in. This was a person who thought ahead, and I liked that.

She came over and stood beside me and Roy until the bartender brought over the sack of guns and handed them to me. They were heavy as hell but I couldn't show nobody no strain, so I put my whole body into it and we strolled out of the place. As we went through the doors,

Roy turned to me, pointed the barrel of his gun toward the girl, and said, "Who might this be?"

I laughed. I laughed right out loud because I was so happy to still be alive, and because I didn't have to make believe those guns were not heavy no more.

"Why, this is my new deputy," I said.

"Your what?"

"This is Andy Colvin," I said, "and she's my new deputy."

"Colvin?" said Roy. "Colvin? Hey, I think I know your daddy."

★ 7 ★

There was hell to pay, of course. While I was still eating breakfast the next morning, two of the town council came to "invite" me to an emergency meeting in the back of Tom's dry-goods store "as soon as possible."

They stood there for a minute like they were expecting me to get right up and go with them, and I guess I would have done it if Mrs. Davis hadn't at that second brought the usual big plate to the table with three fried eggs, a pile of browned potatoes, and two thick slices of fried bread.

"I'll be over as soon as I finish here," I told them, and busted the first yolk with my fork. That lady sure knew how to fry eggs, turning them over for just a few seconds so there wasn't no runny, gooey white parts to make your stomach all queasy, but the yolk was still soft enough to spread out over the plate into the potatoes and the edges of the bread. I think I liked breakfast best of all the meals.

They stood there for another minute watching me chew away, and when Mrs. Davis didn't invite them to have a cup of coffee with us, they finally said they'd see me at the store as soon as possible and left. I was kind of surprised by her not being more friendly toward them, but she must have had her reasons. Once while we were eating, which was really the only time we spent together, I had mentioned the town council and she said, "Don't count on them for anything, whether it's trouble or need." It must have had something to do with when her husband was sheriff or maybe when he was killed, but she didn't say anything more, and I never like to pry when it's a matter causing hurt to anybody.

All five of them were waiting in the back of the dry-goods store, which meant that they must have considered the matter really important because they all had their regular businesses to attend to. They got right down to it.

"What happened last night at the Paris France Saloon?" the skinny one, whose name was Will Jenkins, asked right off.

I told them from the moment I heard the first shots until Roy and me and Andy went out the swinging doors again.

"That's kind of the way I heard it from Elmer Twilley," said Tom Kraft, the dry-goods-store owner. "He was there for the whole thing, and he said the Barron hands could of killed somebody the way they were carrying on."

The Barron hands. Miss Amy's men. Or Crutchfield's men. I had been so stirred up the night before that I hadn't asked Roy if he knew who that gang might have been. I had figured they were trail-herd people who were passing through, but it looked like I had made some acquaintances who were going to be around for a spell.

"That Stark is a bad man," said Mr. Kane, who was a lawyer, which was strange because he usually talked less than anybody and you expect a lawyer to spout off.

"Who's Stark?" I asked, even though I had already figured out the answer.

"He's the foreman," said Kane, "and we've complained to Crutchfield about the way his people carry on in town, especially Stark, but as far as I know, he's never even tried to do anything about it. 'My boys have to let off steam,' he told Tom here the last time he was in the store with his wife."

His wife. Miss Amy. Miss Amy Barron. Mrs. Amy Crutchfield.

"Well, thank God nobody was killed," said Jenkins, "but that's not what we're here to talk about. What has us disturbed is this young woman you seem to be involved with. Twilley says he heard you tell Roy Findley as you went out the door that she was your new deputy.''

Findley. Roy's last name was Findley. Here I'd known him all this time, but this was the first one where somebody used his last name. It was like with me. Everybody thought my last name was Jory. But no one, not even Mrs. Davis, had ever asked me what my other name might be. I guess it's because Jory is so easy to say that they fall into it naturallike.

"That's just what she is," I told them.

Three of them started to open their mouths, but Lawyer Kane beat them to the punch.

"Who is she?" he asked.

"Name's Andy Colvin," I told him. He thought that over for a second.

"Her father own that tiny spread to the west of town?" he asked.

I nodded at him.

"Colvin?" asked Jenkins. "Is he that drunk who fell into the fire pond that time and would have drowned if Herb Davis hadn't pulled him out?" He got two nods in response to that question.

"Never mind about that," said Tom Kraft. "The thing we're here to talk about is you saying that a girl was going to be your deputy. Can't have that. Under no circumstances can we have that. I can understand your being a bit wrought up over what happened last night and grateful to her for what she done, but we can't have that. We just can't have that."

"That's what we're going to have," I told him.

Then all of them but Lawyer Kane started shouting at me to the point where Mrs. Kraft came from the front of the store to shush them up because the women customers were getting nervous. I just stood there waiting for the storm to break, my eyes on Lawyer Kane because he wasn't yelling and I figured him to say something sensible when the din died down. They finally ran out of breath or broke under Mrs. Kraft's shushing, and Kane took his turn.

"You want to give us some reasons why you feel this girl should be your deputy?" he asked. "But first let me tell you that it isn't just us you'll have to convince. You're going to have to persuade the whole town to accept a woman as a deputy, and you'd probably have more trouble with the women about that than the men. It's something I never heard of anywhere, and I'm even amazed that you thought of doing anything so against civilized society's rules. I'll tell you this. Your mind obviously runs deeper than I gave it credit for."

I couldn't tell if he was praising me or chopping me for dog meat. "Never trust a lawyer," my pa had told me once. "Their words don't always mean what their mouths are saying."

"Here's the way I look at it," I told them. "I put posters up everywhere looking for a deputy and not one man stepped forward. And then things went along so easy that I thought maybe I didn't even need a deputy, that I could handle everything by myself. Maybe it was because the weather was so wet and not too many ranch hands or trail herders have been passing through. But last night showed me different. This was the first time a bunch came in and they went and put that lady to shame and threatened the lives and safety of everybody present."

"You couldn't put that lady to shame," said Jenkins. "That's her business and those are the chances she takes. You can't use her for an excuse."

"I'm not making any excuses," I told him. "I'm giving you reasons. And while we're at it, and while I'm sheriff, nobody, I don't care what they do for a living, is going to be put through that kind of thing without me taking some action. A human being is a human being, my pa used to tell me, and that's one of the laws I go by."

"Never mind all that," said Kraft. "Get to the deputy."

"All right. If it wasn't for that deputy, I wouldn't be standing here talking to you right now. I'd either be dead or beat into fresh chicken manure or 'shamed so that I would be out of town and gone from here forever. There was no way that only one man could have handled that bunch by himself. I'm pretty good with guns, but nobody is that good or that fast or that lucky. I was dead. And that girl saved my life. She told me she'd been following me around so she could show me what she could do, and she sure did. Every way to Sunday. She not only was in the right place at the right time for me, but she also had enough iron inside her to make the play that saved my life. You probably heard what she did with that load from her first barrel. She put a hole between the toes of that whatever-his-name-is. And she had the second barrel full of nailheads to take out the rest. That girl knows guns and knows how to use them. When she first came to me, I felt exactly about her and it the way you do. But she convinced me. I'm baptized. I'm a believer. And she's the one I want for my deputy.''

"What if we say you can't have her?" said Kane.

"Then you don't have me either. It wasn't by chance that your last two sheriffs got killed or beat to a frazzle. This town looks pretty quiet when you can just hear the dogs barking, but when the men start to howl, it's a stampede.''

"You're telling us," said Kane, "that if we don't hire this girl, you will resign your post of sheriff.''

"That's what I'm telling you, and you can have the badge right here and now and appoint yourself a new sheriff on the spot.''

"You know we can't get anybody to take the job," said Kraft, his jowly face all red and streaked with white.

"That's none of my business," I told him. "I'm just telling you what I need to protect the lives of the citizens of this town and my own life as well. Your lives went on pretty much as usual when Herb Davis got killed. The problems of his wife and child probably didn't bother you one bit. 'What a pity,' you probably said, and let it go at that. And if I get myself killed, it won't make that much difference to you either. The town will get pushed around for a spell but eventually you'll have another fool come along who'll take on the job because he needs it real bad or don't know no better. You're the ones who called this meeting, so you'll have to make up your minds here and now. Either she stays or we both go.''

''Where's the girl now?'' asked Kane.

''I told her she could put her bedroll down on the jail floor last night because it was too late and dark for her to be riding off home.''

''Well, gentlemen,'' said Kane, ''I for one don't see any need to discuss this matter further. I'm prepared to vote.''

Nobody said nothing and it might have stayed that way forever if Kane hadn't kept going.

''All those in favor of hiring this . . . this . . . Colvin woman as deputy sheriff please signify by raising his right hand.''

Kane, Kraft, and Jenkins put their hands up immediate, but the other two, Alf Landon, and one who I only knew as Brecht, hesitated a few seconds before they followed suit.

''Then it's unanimous,'' Kane said, smiling at me. ''You've got your new deputy.''

''One more thing,'' I told them.

''What's that?''

''Since Andy's going to be doing the work of two deputies, I want her to get more money than the usual deputy would get.''

''Out of the question,'' Landon said.

''How much more do you figure, Sheriff?'' asked Kane.

''I was thinking of something like eighty dollars instead of fifty,'' I told them, knowing we were going to be somewhere in the middle of that. We ended up with her getting sixty-five, which I considered fair until I saw how she worked out.

''Don't forget,'' said Landon again just as everybody was starting to get up. ''We'll be watching her, we'll be watching the two of you like hawks. And if she can't handle the job, it'll mean you can't handle the job either, and we can fire the two of you just as easy as we hired.''

"Fair enough," I told them. ''We ain't looking for nor expecting no favors. You do your part and we'll do ours.''

I stopped in the store to buy some cheese and crackers and a can of peaches to bring over to Andy at the jail because I figured she would sit tight there until I come over.

Mrs. Kraft kept looking at me funny as she was cutting a chunk off the block. I wondered if it was because she knew about what had happened the night before, or because she had heard through the door that I had hired on a girl as deputy.

I knew for sure that the town would think I was peculiar.

As a matter of fact, I thought that maybe they could be right.

★ 8 ★

You know, it wouldn't be a bad idea if someday somebody started a school where they would train you to be a sheriff. Or if somebody would write a book that would lay it out for you, one, two, three. Here I was teaching Andy to be a sheriff, and all I knew about it was what the town council told me they expected and what I had picked up on my own after blundering around for a while. In the big cities back East they have all kinds of police scattered around, a drummer told me once, and I suppose the new ones learn from the old ones. But the sheriff before me, Mrs. Davis' husband, had been killed and couldn't say nothing, and when I went to see the man who was sheriff before Davis, his wife wouldn't even let me in the house.

"We don't want no more trouble," she told me, and I couldn't say nothing about it when there he was sitting in a chair at the back of the kitchen with one eye having a patch over it and the other just open a little slit. I had made up my mind then and there that I was going to teach Andy the few things I did know and then maybe together we could learn some more. We didn't want no patches over our eyes, nor blinders neither.

The first thing I told her was how we were howdy, smiling sheriffs. She didn't smile at all, that girl, probably because she hadn't had much in her life to smile about. I almost asked her to practice one to see if she could do it, but I wasn't sure if I was serious or maybe just funning a bit, so I decided to wait on something like that. After all, it was the way she worked a shotgun that was important, not whether she could pull back her lips and show her teeth. One of the men who worked for Roy said that him and his wife had a room that Andy could sleep in, and they would give her meals as well. Their house wasn't anywhere near as nice as Mrs. Davis' and it didn't look too clean neither, but Roy said they were nice people and they only wanted seven dollars a week, so all in all it wasn't too bad. Nobody could afford to sleep and take his meals in the hotel on a steady basis, and the one time I did eat there the food was mighty poor pickings.

I had her swear the same oath I took, or at least what I could remember of it, and then I pinned the badge on her shirt. There was a whole bunch of deputy badges in the back of one of the drawers, but what with the rust and everything, you could tell they hadn't been used at all. I wondered if all the towns were like Barronville, with people running wild and sheriffs and marshals getting killed. Sometimes you wondered why God had put people on earth to begin with. According to my pa, it was so He could have something to laugh about, but that didn't make much sense to me now that I was growed up. I had come across more good people than bad ones, so I suppose that counted for something.

After Andy had eaten some cheese and crackers, we lugged her stuff over to the Newman house where she was going to live. She hadn't wanted the peaches, so I finished those off while she was rolling up her bed sack. Gawd, but I liked peaches.

When we started our official walk, it was like the first day when I had done it alone. I was back to square one. Not one person said howdy or smiled back at us, and when we passed them and I looked around, they were all there staring at us. And the lawyer was right. I could tell by the looks on the women's faces that they were more than upset about the new deputy—they were mad.

To tell the truth, I felt kind of strange drifting through town with a girl by my side who was the deputy sheriff and carrying a shotgun slung over her shoulder. But every time one of those thoughts crossed my mind, I would also think about what had happened the night before, and I was grateful to be alive and have somebody like this to walk by my side and cover my back.

I was acting like everything was normal, saying "Howdy" and smiling even though nobody was howdying or smiling back. Andy was stiff as a board, looking straight ahead and holding her gun strap so hard that I could see the white of her knuckles through the dirt. I was going to have to do something about getting her cleaned up because you couldn't have your deputy going around looking like a line rider. Mrs. Davis kept all my clothes pretty neat and clean, but I doubted that Mrs. Newman would be doing likewise for Andy. Especially because I didn't think Andy had another set to change off to while her originals were being washed. I had asked Tom Kraft to get Andy some of her pay in advance like they had done for me, and then she could go buy what she needed. Like new pants. I almost smiled at that. That girl didn't have one thing that a woman wears. Hell, if she was a little taller and filled out more, I could have lent her some of my new clothes.

We strolled the town twice instead of just once, with me showing which doors had to be checked and what alleys looked into and what saloons had the most fights and all that. It was really strange telling these things to a girl, pointing out where she might find trouble or could get herself killed. How would I feel if something happened to her when she did the things I was telling her had to be done? Maybe this thing wasn't going to work out now that I could see it in the broad daylight. Or maybe because there were the two of us instead of just me that I felt like we were some kind of parade going through town, except that nobody seemed to be celebrating or waving flags at us.

I had told Mrs. Davis at breakfast some of what had happened the night before and how I had hired on Andy as deputy. At first she seemed as shocked as everybody else and didn't say nothing, but then she told me to bring Andy to the noon meal because she would like to meet her.

After our double walking tour, we spent some time cleaning our guns at the jail. Andy's rifle was one of those Spencers that was used by the Union boys in the war, and she could load seven rounds in there at a crack. Her daddy had won it in a poker game, and although it had seen plenty of use, she treated it like it was her firstborn child. Those carbines usually weren't that good at a distance, but she said she could hit anything she aimed at even if it was on the moon. A boy from Tennessee who was in the war once told me that the Spencer was a gun "you could load on Sunday and shoot it all week," and I wondered how it would do against my Winchester. Which reminded me that we had to get some target shooting in soon because it had been too long since I had last done it, and I was interested in seeing if Andy could do as well with the carbine as she could with the shotgun.

Saturday night wasn't that far away, and we might be having Barron hands paying another visit. They had sent one man in to pick up their guns, one I hadn't seen at the saloon that night. At first I thought about telling him that each one would have to come in and pick up his gun on his own, but then I figured that could get complicated and let it go.

My stomach told me it was nigh on noon, so we put away our rags and oil and started out for the Davis house. One of the things about being a sheriff was that you had a lot of time to kill. In between killings, I guess. Mostly you stood or walked around trying to make the time pass, but when trouble started, it made up for all the sitting back. I didn't think I would like to do this kind of job for too long a time, but right then I was happy I was getting good wages and piling up a little money for whatever I might want to do next in my life.

That whole house smelled of stew cooking when we walked in, and it almost made me giddy, as Mrs. Jordan used to say. I'd had second thoughts about Mrs. Jordan's

cooking as compared to that of Mrs. Davis. When it came
to stew, Mrs. Davis was the best, but her pies and cakes
were just a touch behind those of Mrs. Jordan. You got to
give credit where it's due in this world.

If I'd thought Andy was stiff up to then, it was nothing
compared to how she was when we came into the house
and I introduced the lady and my deputy. It was funny but
at first I was thinking in terms of two ladies, but then it
came to me that Andy was more than just a lady, not that
there's nothing wrong with being that, but that she was a
town official and charged with keeping the peace no matter
who broke it. Tom Kraft had muttered to me that he hoped
this wasn't going to give none of the women ideas that
they could run for town council or anything like that. That
might not be such a bad idea. My pa had told me stories
about ladies who were queens and were in charge of whole
countries, and how some of them had done a real fine job.

Mrs. Davis asked Andy if she wanted to wash up and
Andy told her no, and I could see Mrs. Davis looking at
the dirt on Andy's hands and the smudge on her neck. On
our second walk of the town, Andy had told me that she
had to go somewhere for a spell and I asked her where and
she didn't look at me, just stood there, and I finally said
she could when I realized she wasn't going to say any
more, and then I saw her going into the privy in the back
of Roy's saloon, and I thought how dumb I had been and
how I had to make provision for working with a woman.
But we did have to do something about getting her a bath.

There was a fresh-baked bread to go with the stew and I
sopped up every bit of that gravy so that the plate looked
like it had already been washed. Then we had an apple pie
to go with the coffee. Andy ate slow and steady but not that
much when you got right down to it. Which maybe ac-
counted for her being so skinny. She also kept her eyes on
her dish and didn't even look up when Mrs. Davis asked
her questions, which were the usual things for two strangers, like about her family and the ranch and things like
that. Andy answered by either one or two words, never as

much as three, and some questions she didn't answer at all, letting me or Mrs. Davis pick up the slack. It was like we were eating with some wild critter who wants the food you leave out but is ready to jump and run the instant you take a step toward her.

Her manners were right up to snuff when we left, though. She thanked Mrs. Davis for the nice meal and said she had enjoyed meeting her and then reached over and mushed her hand through the hair on top of Todd's head. It looked for a second like she was almost going to smile when she did that, but she turned her back to go and I couldn't tell if it had happened or not.

What with me being so full of food and the sun shining and not wanting to go back into that stuffy jailhouse, I decided we would take one more walk through the town and see what Andy remembered about the duties of a peace officer. Besides, I figured that once people got used to seeing her around, they might ease up a bit and figure it wasn't so bad having a female deputy. I didn't howdy or smile at anybody this time because my legs were a little tired from all the walking we had done, and I guess I was somewhat peeved at the town for taking this attitude. But then again, they didn't have any idea how it had felt to know you are dead and then be brought to life again. There wasn't no shortcut to getting them used to Andy; they'd have to learn the long way.

There was a wagon outside of the dry-goods store with a Mexican leaning against it, but I would have gone right by if he hadn't stepped out in front of me so that I had to stop or run him over.

"Mr. Jory?" he asked, giving my name that soft slither you hear from people who speak both Mex and American.

I looked down at him and realized right away that he was somebody I should know, but he didn't give me a chance to pull it out of the hat.

"Valdez," he said. "It's Valdez, Mr. Jory."

Jocko, the man who taught me the guns, used to say that he couldn't tell one Mexican from another, that they all

looked alike to him, and I don't know how many others
I've heard say that very thing, usually people I didn't
much cotton to on their own. I liked Jocko and was sorry
when he was killed, but there were some things about him
that bothered me, one of which was his attitude toward
Mexicans. I've never had any trouble telling one from the
other. All of their faces are different, and the way they
walk and talk and act are all different. There were some
Mexicans I had come across that I didn't like, but not
more than I didn't like everybody, if you know what I
mean. The reason I didn't know it was Valdez at first was
that I hadn't seen him in two years and we hadn't been that
friendly to begin with. He was one of the horse wranglers
at the Barron ranch, but most of my time had been spent
with Pedro Iglesias, the head wrangler. But I instantly
remembered how friendly Juan had been the few times we
did spend some time together, and it was good to see him.
I introduced him to Andy and asked him how things were
going, but as he opened his mouth to answer me, he
looked over my shoulder and stopped for a second.

"You can ask the *señora* herself, Mr. Jory," he said,
and I turned to see Amy Barron coming out of the store
with a pot under her arm. She had changed, put on a little
weight, and there was a different look on her face, one that
had frown lines in it. There was also a big black bruise on
her left cheek that was beginning to fade a little but still
looked mean. She was just as pretty, even prettier maybe,
but in a different kind of a way. There was a woman rather
than a girl look to her now. I always had thought of her as
a young colt that's been tamed enough to saddle but was
by no means broken. One of the things that I had liked
about her best was her free and easy way, how each
morning seemed as exciting to her as if it was her birthday. With the way her daddy treated her, each day *was*
like a birthday. It was hard to believe that this giant man
wasn't around no more.

It took her a second, not so much to recognize me as to
realize I was standing there. You could see seven different

looks go across her face before she said anything, and I wondered what was going through her mind as far as I was concerned.

"Jory," she said as she came down the stairs, "I knew you'd be back here someday."

As she came toward me, I wasn't sure what was going to happen. Here we were right out in the open street, so there couldn't be any hugs or nothing like that. Besides, she was a married lady now, and whatever had happened between us before was wiped out by that. She came up so close that I feared for a second that she might even be about to kiss me, but she stopped just short, handed the pot to Valdez and then looked up at me, her chin pointing right at my Adam's apple.

"Daddy's dead," she said, and I could see tears welling up in her eyes, and all I could do was nod to show I knew because I was getting a little wet up there too.

"Roy's living in town here," she said. "He owns the Emily Morgan Saloon."

I nodded again, wondering when she was going to stop being a newspaper.

"Where've you been?" she asked. "I was so angry when you ran off without telling anybody you were going. That was a terrible thing to do to me, Jory." And she stuck that chin forward like she used to do in the old days when she was the princess on the ranch and I was her bodyguard.

"I been everywhere and done everything and now I'm back here for a while," I told her. "It's good to see you, Miss . . . Mrs. Amy."

"So you even know about that?" she said. "I've got no surprises for you. What's that badge?"

"I took me on the job of sheriff for a while," I said. "They needed one bad and I needed a job just as much."

"Sheriff!" she said. "You're the sheriff of Barronville?"

"Right," I told her, "and this is my new deputy, Andy Colvin."

Amy hadn't been paying attention to anybody but me,

so when she turned to look at Andy, her mouth dropped
open.

"But this is a girl," she said. "You can't have a girl for
a deputy."

"I can and do," I told her. "New times are coming in,
Miss Amy."

Both women were kind of acting like the other one
wasn't there, neither even tipping her head to show that an
introduction had been made. There wasn't nothing I could
do about Miss Amy, because she had always done whatever she wanted, but Andy was working for me now, and
she had already forgotten we were howdy, smiling sheriffs. Gawdamighty!

"Jory," said Miss Amy, turning back to me, "I want
you to come to dinner tomorrow night so you can meet my
husband and tell me everything that's happened to you."

"Well, I don't know about that," I told her. "I've got
my official duties and—"

"I won't take no for an answer," she said in her old
Amy way, turning and getting ready to have Juan help her
up on the wagon. "I'm going to expect you to be there,
and that means you better be there."

I didn't know what to say, so I said the thing that had
been at the back of my mind ever since I'd seen her.
"How'd you get that bruise on your cheek?" I asked her.

"I fell off a horse," she said, nodding to Juan, who
whapped the horses with the reins and got them going.

I watched them bumping down the road for a spell, all
disturbed about seeing her again and feeling that all kinds
of things were wrong. That girl never fell off a horse in
her life. She wouldn't know how to fall off a horse even if
someone asked her to.

★ 9 ★

There was a fine mist falling when we took our tour of the town next morning, and hardly anybody was stirring who didn't have to. Things had been so quiet the night before that Andy and I finished the evening round in no more than fifteen minutes. I kept wondering if it would ever be safe to have her make the nighttime circle by herself. On Saturday nights, when the ranch hands came in for their regular drunk and whatever, the two of us would be like Siamese twins so that we would both have our backs covered. The same when a trail herd went through on its way north. But during the week, except for the home-grown drunks, gamblers and troublemakers, who were always more talk than action, things were so quiet that sometimes you almost wished for trouble. That's dumb, isn't it? Wishing for trouble. But what good is an army if it ain't off fighting somewhere? And what good is a sheriff if he ain't got any real sheriffing to do?

Andy had handled her first dog problem just before suppertime. A dog owned by a man named Nicholas had bitten the son of a man named Butler. So Butler had gotten his shotgun and blown the Nicholas dog into more pieces than you'd care to count. And then Nicholas had gotten his shotgun and went looking for Butler.

It was Mrs. Nicholas who came to us and reported what was going on. She said she didn't want her husband to be hung because of a dog, and would we please stop it before it went any further. So me and Andy had split up to cover the whole town, and she was the one who found Nicholas roaming the streets, swearing big oaths and yelling that nobody was going to shoot his "goddamned dog."

When I came upon them, Andy was talking quietly to Nicholas, and she'd already persuaded him to break the gun and pull out the shells. When I got close enough to hear, she was saying as how a dog bite could kill somebody if the animal was crazy and how would he like it if a dog bit one of his kids.

"He didn't have no right to shoot my dog," said Nicholas. "If need be, I would of shot him myself, but that don't mean that just anybody can shoot my dog."

"You're right about that," said Andy. "The proper thing would have been for him to tell the sheriff, and then the sheriff would have taken the right action. But that boy's got a bad bite, Mr. Nicholas, and you can understand how a father might go off half-cocked on something like this. Now, why don't we go over to the Butler house and see how the boy is doing, and then you and Mr. Butler can talk it out a bit? Ain't no sense in letting a grudge fester. You both have to live in this town."

And she took him away to the Butler house, where I suppose they worked things out. I decided to stay out of it and let her have her head on this one. Andy knew I was there and she gave me a nod as they started off, but I could tell she wanted to finish the job by herself and I was just as anxious for her to do it alone as she was. Damned if I might have handled it any better than that. Probably worse. But the thing that pleased me most was seeing that Andy could talk when she needed to. Might even get a smile out of her one of these days.

In any case, we were sitting in the jailhouse doing nothing, and since the town was so quiet, I decided it was a good time to get in some target practice. When I asked Andy if she'd like to ride out someplace and bang some holes in some cans, she said that she would like to check on her house and could we go there for our shooting. It was about a two-hour ride, she said, but it wasn't barely half-past-eight, and we would be back in plenty of time to make another round before I had to ride to the Barron ranch, which was about two hours away in its own right. That was going to be a lot of time in the saddle for a rear end that had softened up in the past few weeks, but my horse could use the exercise after munching away in the livery stable all this time. So I gathered a sack of cans and ammunition and we started off.

Funny about living in a town. You tend to forget how nice it is not to live in a town. But once we hit grassland, it was like a whole new world had opened up, and you could breathe deeper and everything smelled nicer and even though the drizzle was still coming down, you felt like you were in blue-sky country.

We didn't exchange one word that whole ride out, and it wasn't until we hit some fence posts that Andy waved with her hand for me to come up beside her.

"The fence has been cut and the gate pulled down," she said, pointing with her finger where she wanted me to look.

"Where's the house?" I asked.

"About two miles in."

"Lead the way," I told her, and she went into a gallop before me. I had that funny feeling you get in your stomach when you are sure that something is either wrong or about to go wrong. I'd had it many times before when nothing was wrong and nothing went wrong, but this time my stomach had it right. For as we came over a hill, I saw what was left of a small cabin that had been burned right to the ground. The words "ranch house" always meant a big old sprawling place to me, like at the Barron place or at Kingman's, where I had been foreman for a while. But I suppose to Andy and her pa this was ranch house enough, and now somebody had turned it into charcoal and ashes.

She didn't say nothing as we let the horses pick their way down the hill, but there was something different about the way she looked, and I put my right hand down and touched the butt of my gun even though I knew that whatever was going on inside her wasn't directed toward me.

"You have much stuff in there?" I asked her as the horses stopped by themselves before we got very close. Horses don't like the smell of fire; they get skittish when you bring them close.

"Nothing I can't live without," she said. "They killed my daddy and now they killed my house."

"You don't know for sure who did it," I told her.

"You're the sheriff," she said, turning toward me. "Why don't you find out for sure who done it?"

She had me there. Being sheriff was more than walking the town streets and keeping the peace. It was also finding out who done wrong and then making them pay for it. Except I didn't know the first thing about how to go about it. How did you find out who killed a man unless you or somebody else saw him do it? How do you find out who burned down a cabin unless you or somebody else saw it done? I don't see how anybody could figure out who committed a crime unless he saw it with his own eyes. But she was right. I was the sheriff and if anybody should do something about her pa and her house, it was me.

Just then a couple of cows wandered by, big old critters who gave us a long look before munching their way back into the brush again.

"Thought you said your cows had disappeared?" I asked her.

"Those weren't our cows," she said.

"Then whose are they?"

"Maybe they belong to whoever killed my pa, run off our cattle, burned our cabin, cut our fence and knocked down our gate," she said, and there was red in her cheeks that showed she had more going on inside her than what her voice was letting on.

I was thinking of what to say to that when the four cowboys came galloping around the bend and then pulled up short when they caught sight of us. The lead one was a good-looking fellow with a blond mustache, and I could tell by the way he sat his saddle and pranced his horse a bit that he liked to be at the head of a pack. He nudged his horse until he was about five feet away from us, and the other three spread out behind him. They were all wearing six-guns, but there weren't any rifles strapped to their saddles.

Andy was about two feet behind me to the right, and I wished she was on the other side. I felt more comfortable rolling off a horse to the right, but that would put me in her line of fire, so I would have to go to the left. You see, just from looking at these fellows put me in mind of maybe having to shoot. My horse snorted and jerked the reins a bit. Sometimes he was even quicker than I was to recognize when somebody was on the prod, but this time I was right up with him.

Andy had her shotgun slung over her shoulder and her Spencer in its case on her saddle, but if something did happen, it wouldn't be no long-range battle, and I hoped she could get that scattergun going quickly if need be.

"Well," said the blond fellow, "what have we here? It looks like that dangerous sheriff we heard about and his deputy, Shotgun Annie."

He grinned at us, and you know what, it was a friendly kind of a grin instead of one of those mean ones. You can't go by smiles, of course. In Dodge City I saw a gambler smile at a man and then pull out a derringer from his sleeve and shoot him right in the belly. As soon as the other people in the game realized it was a one-shot gun, they stood up and beat the hell out of that gambler. I don't know how it started, but it sure had one hell of an ending.

"What are you doing out here, Sheriff?" he asked. "I thought you'd be busy in town."

"We're looking to see who might have burned this place down," I said, "and who might have cut the fence and knocked down the gate."

"I couldn't imagine who might have done all that," said the spokesman. "Do you, boys?"

And he turned around and looked at them, and they all shook their heads no and smiled when they were doing it. Except that their smiles didn't look so friendly as the blond man's, and that convinced me that he was the one we had to watch closest.

"Could have been anybody drifting through," he said. "After all, this is free range."

Andy spoke. "This ain't no free range," she said. "This is my land and that was my house, and you're trespassing."

"Trespassing?" said the blond one, putting a look on his face like a woman who just had a chicken jump under her skirt. "If anything, it's Barron land, and you people are the trespassers and we'll thank you kindly to get off it."

"You the ones who cut the fence and did all the other things?" I asked them.

"What if we are?" said one of the men to the left of the blond. "You may have been lucky in town, but that don't mean shit out here."

I almost went for it then. He used that word just because Andy was there, and you didn't use a word like that in front of a woman. But what held me back was that things were now even in my mind. Sure, I thought of Andy as a woman, but just as equal I thought of her as a deputy sheriff, and a deputy sheriff can hear that word without getting in an uproar.

"You going to move out of here," said the blond one, the smile gone from his face, "or are we going to have to do it for you? You ain't in a saloon with twenty people backing you this time?"

Twenty people backing us? My, my, but that story must have changed its details by the time those Barron hands had gotten back to the ranch.

"Let me tell you what's going to move," I said. "You're all going to move your hands up a little higher than they are and unbuckle your gun belts and let the whole thing slide to the ground nice and easy. Then I'm going to take you in for what you did here, and we'll let the town council decide on how you're going to pay for it either in money or your hides."

"You hear that, boys?" said the blond. "Sheriff wants us to drop our guns and go into jail. What do you say about that?"

He started to draw when he came to the word "that," and I threw myself to the left off the horse, hit on my left shoulder, rolled over and came up on my knees with both guns out and shot the blond one as he was trying to move his gun to cover me. I hadn't done that trick in I don't know how long, and I hit on my shoulder harder than I ought and I had also landed in a muddy spot and that made me madder than ever.

I'd heard the boom of Andy's shotgun just as I was rolling off the horse, and as I brought my guns to bear on the other three, I found that there was nothing to shoot at. I don't know what kind of load she had in her shells this time, but two of the others were down on the ground and the third one was just trying to keep his seat on his horse and yelling his lungs out, but he lost the battle and was pitched to the ground right on his head.

I looked back quick at Andy and saw that she was holding the shotgun ready in case the other barrel was needed. Damned if I know how she got that gun off her shoulder and in action so quick, but she had taken care of three while I was only able to do one. Maybe we had things a little mixed up and she had ought to be sheriff and me deputy.

I stood up feeling a little foolish because of the wet mud sticking to me, my heart still racing from working with the guns again after all this time. I walked over to the blond, who was laying there moaning with a hand covering his left shoulder, which had quite a bit of blood coming out of it. I was quite upset. Here I'd gone for the middle of his chest and what I'd done was get him in the shoulder. That had happened to me once before when I was younger, but I'd had two beers beforehand and wasn't feeling good. This

time there was no excuse except that I was out of practice.
Maybe Andy didn't need any, but I sure did.

The other three were barely hurt. The two of them
who'd gone down had a few shotgun pellets in them here
and there, but they were mostly on the ground because
they were afraid to get up. The third one was even luckier
in that he was only knocked out and didn't have a broken
neck or something else bad. I pulled the gun belts off all
four of them, the blond one pissing and moaning and
crying while I was doing his. You know, it's funny, but so
often the ones that act the hardest turn out to be the softest
when the chips are down. This one was great when it was
four against two and one of them a girl, but right now
you'd think the bullet that went through his shoulder had
taken his guts along with it.

"Listen!" I said, loud enough for the wounded one to
stop wailing for a minute and for the two who weren't
knocked out to look at me as quick as they could. "We
ain't going to take you into jail because you're not worth
the trouble, and there ain't no reason why you should be
added to the garbage we already have in town. I'm confis-
cating your guns and I'm warning you not to let me catch
sight of you again. And you tell your boss that I expect
these fences to be strung again and the gate fixed and
money paid for the loss of the cabin, and I want your cattle
to hell out of here. Or else he will be dealing with the law
on the matter. Now get your friend on a horse and take
him where he can get fixed up."

It took them a while to catch their horses, and finally
Andy had to round up two of the critters. Then they had to
load the blond one on his animal and ride one on each side
to keep him from falling off. They didn't say nothing this
whole time. I could imagine what they were thinking, but
you knew they weren't going to open their mouths until
they got to a place where they were sure we couldn't hear
them.

"That was nice moving," I told Andy when we couldn't

see the four of them anymore. "How the devil did you get that gun 'round and off so quick?"

She had it up on her shoulder with the sling again, and as I was asking, her hand moved almost quicker than I could see and the gun was pointing just to the side of me. She was as fast getting that shotgun around as I was pulling a handgun. This wasn't no fluke of nature; God gave me this deputy.

"Okay," I said, "where was it you had in mind for us to do some target shooting?"

She looked at me surprised. I was so pleased at getting a different look on her face that it took me a second to wonder what she was wondering about.

"You still want to go target shooting?" she said.

"Hell, yes," I said, so wrought up that I was using a cuss word in front of her myself. "My shot was a good eight inches off where I wanted it to go. If it keeps up like that, I may have to change to a shotgun myself."

"Can you teach me how to go off a horse like that and come up shooting?" she asked.

"That could be done," I told her. "I could use a little practice at that myself. But let's do it on high ground."

"Before we do," she said, "can we go out there and check my daddy's grave?"

The look on her face was really different this time. I wondered what went on inside that head all the time. But then again, I didn't know what went on inside my head all the time.

★ 10 ★

We got back to Barronville about half-past-two, and I told Andy to tour the town to see that everything had gone all right while we were away. If she wanted me, I was going to be at the Davis house for a short while and then probably the bathhouse. She nodded and went on her way.

I told the boy at the livery stable to give the black a good rub because we still had a lot more riding to do that day. As I walked to the Davis house, I thought on the shooting practice me and Andy had done. Damned if she wasn't as good or better with that rifle than she was with the shotgun. She'd bounced those cans from a distance where I could barely make them out, let alone hit them. It's a good thing I ain't the kind of person who gets upset when someone bests them at something, especially when it's a girl. Well, maybe I am a little bit of that kind of person because my stomach gave a few twitches when my shots missed the cans clean and then Andy blew them into the air. One time, and if I hadn't seen it I wouldn't have believed it, she put a can in the air and then hit it while it was up there. That ain't shooting; that's magic.

I strapped on her one of the six-guns we took from the Barron hands, and tried to teach her how to draw, but she was all fingers and thumbs. Then I had her shoot at the cans from close up, but she didn't hit one of them no matter how many times she banged away. I've got to admit it made me feel a little better about the whole thing. I'm a pretty good shot with a rifle, better than most men, so I didn't feel that bad about Andy outshooting me there. As a matter of fact, it made me kind of proud. After all, I had picked her and she was my deputy.

While I was getting the gun belt on her, I had to stand pretty close and she smelled real strong, so I decided to take the bull by the horns and put it right to her.

"You bought any new clothes with the money the town gave you?" I asked.

"Don't need none," she said. "These ain't wore out yet."

"That ain't what I'm talking about," I told her. "A deputy's got to be neat and clean at all times, except maybe when he throws himself in the mud if need be, so that means he has to change his clothes once in a while so he can take a bath and then put on clean ones while his old ones are being washed."

"All right," she said.

Here I'd been all set for an argument and she'd just nodded her head and that was the end of that. Of course, the way she could shoot and the kind of backbone she had, I would have allowed her to stay dirty if she'd been stubborn about it, but she must have figured that if the sheriff wanted his deputy to be clean and neat, that was the way it was going to be.

The sheriff at that moment wasn't clean and neat himself, so I went back to the Davis house to get some clothes to take to the bathhouse with me. Mrs. Davis was ironing something frilly on the kitchen table, and when she saw me come out of my room with the clothes, she asked where I was going.

"To the bathhouse," I said.

"I hate to see you spend all that money there," she said. "Why don't I heat up some water and bring in the tub and you can bathe right here in the kitchen without it costing you anything."

"That would be too much trouble for you," I said. "I don't mind spending the money."

But she would have her way, and when she asked if I'd

had my noon meal, I told her no and she said she would make me something while the water was heating. The trouble at the Colvin place and the target shooting had gotten me so het up that I'd plumb forgot about eating, which some folks I know would have considered a miracle to equal the parting of the Red Sea or Jesus walking on the water, both of which events my pa used to relish talking about. He wasn't what you would call a true believer.

So we filled all the pots and kettles and put them on the stove, and then I dragged in the wooden tub, which was one of the smallest I had ever seen and made me wonder if I would fit in it to begin with. But I ate some bread and cold meat and watched Mrs. Davis iron and could see Todd through the open door playing with something in the back yard. The pots were beginning to bubble and the kettle to steam by the time I had finished, and I put some cold water in the tub and then some hot water and mixed it so it seemed just right for a bath.

Mrs. Davis kept on ironing while I was doing all this and didn't stop when I had the tub ready for use. I didn't know what to say, so I just stood there waiting.

She finally looked up. "Oh," she said, "are you all ready? Then I'll just go out back and see what Todd is up to."

She went out and closed the door behind her, so I skinned out of my clothes and stepped into the tub. You know, it's always the case. The water feels just fine to your hand, but when you go to stick your ass in it, it's hot enough to make you wince. Once you get in, it's not too bad, but those first few minutes make you shrivel a bit.

The tub was so small that the water barely came up to my belly button, so I reached out to the table where Mrs. Davis had put a big towel and a little cloth and took the rag and started to scrub the upper part of my body. But when I reached out to the table again to get the soap, it wasn't there. I looked all around the room but couldn't spot it for beans. Damn! I like to get myself all soapy and then lay there in the soapy water and soak away all the little aches that came this time from riding almost five hours when I hadn't been on a horse in over two weeks.

The back door opened a bit and Mrs. Davis said, "Jory, is everything all right?"

"Yes, ma'am, I told her."

"Did I remember to put soap out for you?"

I didn't know what to say, just sat there in the water like a bullfrog on a pad.

"Jory?"

"Yes, ma'am."

"Is the soap there?"

"No, ma'am, it isn't."

"Oh, Lord," she said, opening the door and coming right into the kitchen, "sometimes I think I'd lose my head if it wasn't attached to my body."

She went to the cabinet by the sink and pulled out a large chunk of brown soap that she'd made the week before and brought it over to me.

"My," she said, "you're a little big for that tub. We had a bigger one before, but after Herbert died, I traded it for this one because I couldn't handle the other one by myself."

"Thank you, ma'am," I said, taking the soap and then sitting there waiting for her to go back out into the yard. I could feel the red heat climbing up into my face.

"You can barely move in that thing," she said, giving a laugh that was close to a giggle. Somehow I had never thought of Mrs. Davis as the giggling type. She laughed sometimes over something that Todd did or said, but I didn't have no idea how she might have laughed over my present predicament.

"Here," she said, "you give me that cloth and I'll scrub your upper parts and then rinse you off."

"Oh, I can do that fine, ma'am," I said, lifting my arm to show her and causing water to spill over the sides onto the floor.

"See," she said, "see what happens. You just give me that cloth and I'll have you done in a minute." And she took the cloth and the soap and went to work on my chest.

Gawd. You know what happened when that woman bent over me and started to scrub and I could see her things bobbing under the dress and her hands felt so soft and smooth on my body with the hard scrubbing with the rough cloth, and try as I did not to, it happened to me anyway. I kept my hands between my legs to try to cover it up, but she kept moving my arms to get at various places, and her face was looking right down in that water while she was doing it. I don't know how long it went on, but it seemed forever. Finally, she poured some clean water over my back and chest and stood back.

"There," she said, "that looks fine. And you didn't have to pay a dollar at the bathhouse."

I looked at her standing there with her face all pink from the scrubbing and some of her hair fallen down because of the steam, and I thought how pretty she looked and how nice it would be to hold and kiss a woman like that if only she wasn't so old.

"Is there anything else I can do?" she asked, giving that funny giggle again.

"No, ma'am," I said. "As soon as you go back outside, I'll get out of here and get dressed again."

"Oh," she said. "All right. If that's what you want." And she went out and closed the door.

I dried off and dressed and started carrying buckets of water outside till I could get the tub light enough to take out. Mrs. Davis was sitting on the ground watching Todd play with his whittled wooden horse, and she didn't look up once all the while I was carrying the water out. I went back in and dried up the floor with the towel and folded it neat and put it back on the table. Then I went out back again and walked over to where she was sitting. At first she didn't look up at me, but when I just stood there, she finally lifted her face in my direction. Her eyes looked wet, like she'd been crying, but I figured she was just a little sweaty from working over the hot water.

"I'm going out to the Barron place to eat tonight," I told her, "so don't hold supper for me."

"The Barron place?" she said, her voice rising. "Why are you going out there?"

"I bumped into Miss Amy in front of the dry-goods store yesterday," I said, "and she invited me out to talk over old times and meet her new husband."

"But, Jory," said Mrs. Davis, "you had all that trouble with the Barron people the other night. You can't go out there."

Gawdamighty, I had to be the dumbest person in the world. Somehow I had never connected Miss Amy with what had gone on with the Barron hands in the saloon or with the other Barron hands that very morning. I wouldn't be what you would call the most popular person with the people who lived in the Barron bunkhouse. Except they had to realize that I was only doing my duty. But they were a mean bunch, and it was almost as if somebody had put them on the prod against me. It would be downright foolish to go by myself right into the middle of them, like a lamb going to visit a den of wolves.

But Miss Amy had invited me and she wouldn't let no foolishness take place. Except she probably didn't know what had happened in the saloon and couldn't know what had happened that very day. It would be crazy to go out there.

But then again, I had accepted her invitation and it wouldn't be polite to back out now. And if word got out that the sheriff was feared to go out to the Barron place because he'd had a run in with some of the hands, nobody would have no respect for me after that. No matter what I did, I was in trouble.

But then there was me. How would I feel about myself if I didn't go out there? The only reason not to go was because there might be trouble with the hands, and if I was afraid to face them there, then maybe I would start being afraid to face them anywhere. No, no matter if I got killed or whatever, I had to eat dinner at the Barron ranch that night. No two ways about it.

"Shucks," I told Mrs. Davis, "I just had a little run-in

with those people. Nothing to get excited about. Besides, Miss Amy invited me and those hands aren't going to do nothing when I'm there as a friend of the family."

"I wouldn't trust any of those Barrons," said Mrs. Davis, her voice getting a little shrill, enough so that Todd stopped playing with his horse and was looking up at her a little fearful. "Herbert was killed right after he'd had some trouble with that foreman, that Stark person. I've always felt that he had something to do with it."

"He's trouble, all right," I said, "but I don't know how brave he is without a whole gang in back of him."

"That's the point exactly," said Mrs. Davis. "Out there he will have a gang of men behind him. And you'll be riding home in the dark."

"I have to go out there," I told her. "There are a lot of reasons I can't explain, maybe even to myself, but I've got to go out there."

"Then take some people with you," she said. "Take Andy. Me! I'll go out there with you."

"She only invited me to dinner," I said. "If I showed up with a whole bunch of people, they'd think it strange. I'll be fine."

"Well," she said, "I can see I can't change your mind. But I'm not going to bed until you're back here and I don't care what time it is."

"Now, that's going to make me feel bad," I said, "and I'll be worrying all through dinner that I'm keeping you up. If you do what you say, I'm going to have to leave there real early so's you can get your beauty sleep."

"Good," she said. "I'll count on that."

I'd told the livery boy what time I was coming back and he had the black all saddled and ready to go when I got there. You could tell that the son of a gun was happy to be working again, and for a second I thought he was going to give me a buck or two to show how glad he was. But then he just settled into an easy pace and we were on our way to the Barron ranch.

I was kind of excited about going there after being away

for two years. I wondered if Conchita was still there, and I thought of how she was the first woman to show me how to act like a man. Goddamn, but she had big ones. Mrs. Davis' were lady-size and Andy didn't seem to have none at all, but Conchita had more than enough to go around and then some. It was hurting to ride and I wondered why the stiffness hadn't worked out, and then I realized that my problem came from Mrs. Davis helping me with my bath. Gawdamighty, she must have thought of me like she did Todd if she felt she had to help me take a bath.

I was thinking all these things because I was trying hard not to think of what I was riding into. I had the cold feeling in my stomach and it wasn't a good one. There was one thing that really bothered me. Was I afraid? Was I afraid to go in there and maybe have to face down who knew how many of the hands? Was I afraid thinking of how I was going to have to ride back in the dark and who knew who would be waiting out there?

I pulled both my guns, spun them twice and shoved them back in the holsters. Twelve bullets. But hell, there could be twenty of them against me. Except that Miss Amy wouldn't allow that. She wouldn't invite me out there to be killed. Of course, if she invited me to stay overnight in my old room, I would be coming back in the daylight. But Mrs. Davis said she was going to wait up, and if I didn't show up, the poor woman would have a conniption. Damn! I couldn't win for losing. But the hand had been dealt and now I had to play it out no matter how the cards fell.

"Jory," I said out loud to myself, "you do get yourself in the most peculiar situations. And one of these days you ain't going to be able to get yourself out."

For the rest of the ride I kept wondering if this might be the one.

★ 11 ★

The sun, which had first showed its face about noon, said it was near four o'clock when I started out on the wagon road to the Barron ranch. It could have been earlier or later because I'm not that good about figuring time by the sun. I have met old-timers who would take a quick look at the sky and tell you almost to the second what time it was. And they could do it on rainy days as well as bright ones. My father had a real gold watch, but he traded it for some whiskey in one of the towns we passed through, and time didn't make no difference to us anyway in those days. I kept thinking I would buy myself a watch if I ever had some extra money, so I would know exactly when something happened or how much time I had before I had to meet somebody. Except that it never made any difference what time something happened because it was going to happen anyway no matter what time it was, and I almost never had to meet anybody, and if I did, I would find them or they would find me one way or another. But I remembered playing with my father's watch, looking at the hands go around and around, and putting it up to my ear so I could hear the ticking, and I thought it would be nice to have one of those to wind each day and take care of. Watches and clocks aren't very useful and probably never will be, but that's true of a lot of the stuff we set store by.

Andy had said she would make the rounds that night, and I told her if there was any trouble she thought she couldn't handle, that she should go to Roy or Tom Kraft and get their help. She just gave me that blank stare when I said that to her. What was amazing was that it didn't bother me none to leave her in charge all by herself because I knew what she could do and never get flustered while she was doing it, no matter what was going on.

I decided to take the wagon road to the Barron ranch even though it would have been quicker across country because I didn't want to get there too early and it was easier for Bones to canter down the middle of the tracks. After a while we started to come on places that I recognized, hills and outcrops and rocks that I had given names to because of their different shapes, and it gave me a stir as we got closer and closer. It didn't get rid of the cold feeling in my belly, but it kind of warmed it down to workable size. Twice I pulled my Colts and gave them a twirl, and it was strange because I hadn't done nothing like that since I was first learning the guns when we had come down to Texas three years before. I used to do it all the time then, pulling on snakes and birds and anything that moved. That was when guns were still fun to me.

Just before we reached the gate of the ranch, I turned off the track and cut across country, so I could come on the place from the back instead of the front. As I topped the hill and looked down at the big house and the barns and the bunkhouse and the Mexicans' shacks, it gave me the strangest feeling I think I ever had. It was like I was shivering from the inside out rather than the way it usually is. The last time I had sat a horse on that spot it felt like I was on top of the world with me being Miss Amy's bodyguard and having a nice room in the house and three meals a day and my choice of horses from the whole remuda. If someone had asked me if I could use one word to describe how I felt about all that at the time, I guess I would have come up with contented. Maybe it had been foolish to run away from it, but sixteen ain't the same as eighteen whether you count up or down.

Didn't seem to be any men near the houses, just the usual Mexican women and kids, so I nudged Bones into

picking his way down the hill. I recognized two of the
women I rode by and gave them a smile and a Mexican
howdy, but not one of them said anything or even smiled
back. The kids were friendlier and shouted and laughed and
waved at me even though they didn't have the slightest
idea who I was. I like kids.

I rode right up to the horse barn, where Valdez and
Pedro Iglesias were both holding up the leg of a big white
horse so they could check something on his hoof, and they
were looking so hard that they didn't hear or see me until
they dropped the hoof back on the ground and stood up to
wipe their hands on their pants.

"Señor Jory," yelled Pedro, "Juan told me you were
back." And he came running over and reached up and
grabbed me by the arm. I slid off the horse to the ground,
and Pedro put both arms around me and we started to
pound each other on the back hard enough to raise a dust
devil.

"Ah, Señor Jory," he said, "I have thought of you
often since you left. When the *jefe* went to God"—both
Pedro and Juan crossed themselves—"and Miss Amy was
left all alone, how we wished you were here to take care of
her. She was like the *ternero* who has wandered away
from the herd and keeps bawling for her mother. Or a
person who is drowning and grabs for whatever is available even if it is just a straw. And before we knew it, she
had married this straw, and now the happy days are gone
from this place and there are no smiles any more, especially from the *señorita*."

I had gotten used to the flowery talk that could go on
forever when the Mexicans got themselves wound up on
something close to their hearts, but what Pedro had just
said only gave me a hint of what I wanted to know about
what was going on at the ranch and in town. Whenever
you mentioned Barron, people just locked their mouths
tight and looked like they wanted to be anywhere but
where they were. Once in a while somebody let something
slip about missing cows or somebody getting killed or the

ranch hands tearing the place apart on Saturday nights, but mostly they were careful. The Barron ranch was big business for the town. I was pretty damn sure that Andy's pa had been done in by Barron people and maybe they had done in Sheriff Davis, too, but it was hard for me to believe that Miss Amy would put up with a bunch of killers running crazy all over the place. Her pa wouldn't have stood it for a minute, and she was cut out of the same block of granite. I knew this girl, had almost died with and for her, had even thought about marrying up with her, and I couldn't, wouldn't believe what I was hearing.

"She's still got you and Valdez and some of the others to take care of her," I said.

"Ah, *señor*, but we are Mexicans. All of the Mexicans are still here, but all of your *compañeros* are gone. When Mr. Roy was hurt and went into town, Señor Crutchfield told all the other gringos to leave too. Then he brought in a whole new bunch from somewhere that he knew before. These people do not like Mexicans, *señor*. They treat us like we are dirt beneath their feet. I am no longer the head wrangler; all my years are washed away. These new . . . But, Señor Jory, I have heard of what happened at the saloon in Barronville, and this very morning four of them returned wounded from wherever they were, and they claimed that you shot at them from the woods and then ran away. It is craziness that you are here. Why are you here?"

"Miss Amy invited me to come out for dinner and meet her new husband," I told him.

"But he is the leader of these *ladrones*," said Pedro, so wrought up that he grabbed both my arms as though I was trying to run away from him. "Even though you are now sheriff, there is no law out here. There is no way to protect you."

"I don't need any protection, Pedro," I said. "Miss Amy wouldn't invite me out here to get myself killed."

"I'm sure she knows nothing about what happened, *señor*," said Valdez. "She would have no idea of the trouble there would be for you. Pedro and I and the others are here if you need help, but these are not regular ranch hands as they were before. These are all men of the gun, such as you are, and although you are the best that I have ever seen, you are one against the many. There can be only one way for such a contest to end. Ride off, *señor*. Go back to town where you have friends and help. Here there is only trouble. Ride off, *señor*.''

Those two had me spooked enough by this time so that I was seriously pondering about how foolish I had been to come out there and that maybe I ought to just skedaddle while my presence was still unknown. Except that it wasn't. All of a sudden there was one of those silences that gives you a prickly feeling on your back, and I turned quickly to find out what was there.

They were there. Six of them. And in the middle was Stark, the foreman, with the unfriendliest smile on his face I had ever had the unpleasure of seeing. The rest of them were smiling, too, but they couldn't come anywhere near Stark on that matter. All of these Barron hands seemed to smile when they were about to do something nasty. Like the one that morning. These were people who pleasured in meanness.

I stepped away from Pedro and Valdez so that they wouldn't be part of whatever was going down. They didn't even have iron on them, and it wasn't their fight in the first place. Pedro and I had been real friendly when I had worked on the ranch, but there wasn't no reason he should get himself killed on my behalf. He had a wife and God knows how many kids, and I'm pretty sure it was much the same with Valdez. I kept moving sideways until there was no chance that the Mexicans would be in the middle of any crossfire. As I was moving, Stark's men were spreading out themselves, just like they'd done in the saloon when we had our first meeting. At least there were only six of them this time, which was not a happy number to be sure, but it came to two bullets apiece in case my aim was still a little off. I looked quick to both sides of me to see which way would be best when I went into the diving roll that Jocko had taught me was the only way you had a chance against more than one gunslinger. Shooters get a little confused when they see a body flying through the air and their shots can go anywhere rather than into you. There was a wagon off to the right side, and if I could get under that after my roll, I could go for their crotches, which was even easier than a head shot.

"Well, Sheriff," said Stark, "who'd have thought we would have the pleasure of meeting you again so quick after the first time."

Gawd, what I wouldn't have given to have had Andy somewhere in the near vicinity with her scattergun loaded and ready. It's bad enough to go against one person, or maybe two, but the kind of odds I was coming up against lately was like a gambler drawing aces and eights. I'd been lucky up to then, but a cat has only so many lives.

"I'm here," I told them, "because the owners of this ranch invited me. I'm not here to make trouble or to get into trouble, but I am an officer of the law and anybody who draws a gun is going to get himself killed or put into jail."

"Why would anybody want to draw a gun, Sheriff?" said Stark. "We're all peaceful, law-abiding citizens right here where we belong on our own ranch. You're the one who's come in wearing guns and looking for trouble. And trouble's something we never step away from."

The problem with six of them spread out like they were is that you are never sure which one is going to pull first, so you have to keep your eyes roving all the time, but when you get all the way to the man who's on the end to the left of you, there ain't no way you can see what the man on the right is doing. So, though I never moved my head from the front, one reason being that I thought nobody would draw until Stark made the move or gave the signal, my eyes were going back and forth until I worried that one eye might meet the other eye going the other way and I would end up with crossed eyes forever. That was only one of the little worries, however. There were bigger ones.

Both Pedro and Valdez had slipped away, and I wondered if they were getting away from the trouble or gone to fetch their guns. I hated to think of maybe something happening to them in a fight that wasn't their own, but I must admit that I would have felt a lot better if I knew that they were going to back me up. One against six was a tough mountain to climb; three against six was a little hill.

"Well," I said, tired of all the mouthing that was going on and just about ready to throw myself to the right and come up under that wagon shooting, "I guess it's your move."

"Move?" said Stark. "We're not here to make a move. We're here to deliver a message."

"What's that?" I asked, wondering what kind of craziness they might have in mind.

"We're here to say that the folks in the big house are waiting supper on you and you better hurry up there before everything gets cold."

★ 12 ★

Danged if they didn't escort me all the way over to the big house, walking a little way behind, saying nothing, trying to spook me into looking back to see what they might be up to. I just kept walking ahead like there wasn't nothing on my mind but the sinking sun and what we might be having for supper. But I must admit that I did feel somewhat foolish with all those spurs jangling behind me. It was as if I was a little kid being brought somewhere by grown-ups who weren't part of his family.

A Mexican woman I didn't know was standing on the porch, and when she saw us coming, she turned and hurried into the house. By the time we reached there, Miss Amy was out to greet us, mixed up between saying hello to me and looking strange at the six galoots six paces behind, who turned and went back to where they had come from after giving her a tip of the hat.

"I didn't know you were friendly with any of our crew," she said, holding out her hand for a shake.

"Well," I said, "friendly might not be quite the word. We got acquainted the other night and I think they'd like to get to know me better."

"That's nice," she said. "I'm so glad you came out. How does the place look to you?"

The bruise on her face had faded somewhat, but the dark blotch stood out from her sun-browned face, almost like one of them birthmark things you see on people. I almost asked if I could see the horse that threw her.

"The buildings all look the same, but I don't think I know even one of the white punchers," I told her.

"I don't know some of them that well either," she said. "After Roy got hurt and left, Jasper decided he wanted to start with a whole new crew and brought in several of the men who had been in the army with him. He said we had too many Mexicans, too, but I told him that this was their home and my daddy wouldn't have put up with any of them leaving for one minute."

Her eyes started to shine a bit when she said the word "daddy," and I thought maybe some tears were starting, so I turned toward the west where the sun was getting bigger and redder by the minute.

"I was sure taken back when I heard about your daddy," I said without looking at her. "It wasn't the same as when I lost my own pa, but he was as close to kin as anybody could get."

"He was very fond of you," she said, "and was quite upset when you left without telling him. He was mad at first because that was his way, and then he worried that you didn't have enough money or might get in trouble with your guns."

Up until then I had never figured on getting into trouble with my guns. Just the opposite. I figured that my guns got me out of trouble. But then again, why did I keep trying to give them up? There must have been something deep down in me that knew there was a wrong mixed in. Once, when I had been foreman at the Kingman ranch, I got drunk on brandy with a preacher who was married to Mr. Kingman's sister, and he made me get down on my knees and promise the Lord to "forswear the guns." I'd liked the sound of that so much that I said what he told me to, but life isn't the same when you sober up. If I hadn't used my guns, I would have forsworn my life. The guns were like a bad wife; I was stuck with them.

"I've done all right," I told her. "No need for your daddy to have worried."

"Come on in," she said, her voice clear and steady

again. "Jasper's trying to make the fire burn better. We've been having problems with the draft."

I followed her through the door but stopped dead right there. It was so strange to be seeing all the things I knew so well, the rugs, the big mirror on the wall, the horns mounted on boards, the staircase leading to the second floor. It was like I'd been dead and brought back to life. I might be standing there yet if Miss Amy hadn't called out to me.

That whole thing was nothing compared to how I felt when I walked into the big room because the first thing I saw was Mr. Barron bending down over the fireplace poking at a log. I saw a man they had told me was dead as big as life. I didn't know whether to run toward him or turn around and scoot away. I almost yelled, but I had no air to push it out. All kinds of crazy things flashed through my mind. They had all lied to me about Mr. Barron dying. What I was seeing was a ghost come back to haunt me. I turned to Miss Amy to see if she was seeing what I was seeing, and she certainly was but she didn't seem flustered at all.

"Jasper," she called out, "this is my friend Jory that I told you so much about."

The man turned his head and I saw right away that it wasn't Mr. Barron at all. Mr. Barron was old, somewhere around fifty, and this fellow couldn't have been much more than thirty or so, which is old enough but not like fifty. When he stood up, I could see the reason I was fooled: because he was almost as big as Mr. Barron had been, and there was some look-alike to their faces. There was even the same kind of mustache, bushy and drooping at the ends. The eyes were different. Mr. Barron's were squinty from all his years in the sun, while the ones looking at me were big and blue and almost round.

"Well," he said, holding out his hand and moving toward me, "I finally get to meet the man who has no imperfections. If I had a dollar for every time Amy mentioned your name, I'd be the richest man in Texas. I was beginning to wonder whether you were human or not, but you look pretty human to me."

I took his hand carefully because it's been my experience that big men sometimes like to squeeze extra hard on a shake to make you feel even smaller than you are. My hands are pretty strong from a trick a boxer showed me once in Dodge City. He had this whole box of smooth round rocks, and he'd take one in each hand and squeeze it a hundred times every day. He gave me two of them for nothing, although I don't know if a couple of stones are worth anything unless there is gold or silver in them, but it was still a nice thing to do. I didn't get to practice with them every day, sometimes not for weeks, but when I thought about it, I would haul them out of my pack and do the squeezing while I was riding along or sometimes at night when I wasn't sleepy enough to roll in. And you know what? They did make my hands stronger, right to the point where I can safely shake hands with anybody, even when they catch me by surprise.

But he wasn't one of those who show off, because his shake was nice and steady and polite, and it surprised me so much that I gave him a couple of extra ones after he thought we were all through, and that was a surprise to him because he kept trying to untangle his fingers from mine.

"It's a pleasure to meet you," I told him. Now even as I was saying that, I was wondering in my mind how big a lie I was telling. I was feeling a lot of things but pleasure was not one of them. Some of the stories I had heard about this man had disturbed rather than pleasured me. There had been his firing of Roy after he became hurt. There had been those remarks by people about missing cattle maybe being on the Barron spread. There had been the run-ins with the hands from the Barron ranch, and it has been my experience that you can usually judge a man by the way the people who work for him act. There was the trampling of Andy's pa and the burning down of the cabin and the moving in on the land, and there was the bruise on Miss Amy's face. But I was there as their supper guest, and Miss Amy was standing there all smiling, and he'd greeted me real friendly, and I had no cause to be other than polite. Sometimes there are explanations for the bad things you hear about people, and it turns out that it was just evil gossip to begin with, or there were reasons why they did like they did. Keeping all that in mind, though, I still had a feeling about the man that had nothing to do with pleasure. And I've got to admit this too: knowing that Miss Amy belonged to him, that she slept in his bed each night and spent each day taking care of his wants didn't brighten up my life any to begin with.

"How about a drink after your long ride?" said Crutchfield. "I'm sure you could use a whiskey as much as I could."

"No, thank you," I said. "I don't drink whiskey nor beer much either. But I would welcome a glass of water."

"What?" yelled Crutchfield, turning to look at me with his eyebrows raised on his head and acting like I'd just told him that his pecker was hanging out. "You don't drink whiskey? Why, with all the things I've been hearing about you, I figured you put down a bottle a day."

He was funning me, for sure, but I wasn't clear on whether there might be a little meanness mixed in with it. He was acting the same way Mr. Barron had the first time I met him when Roy recommended I be hired. The old man had poured three glasses of whiskey and when I said I didn't want any, I remember his exact words.

"There's something female about men who don't drink," he had said.

And now this here fellow was saying the same thing without saying the same thing. He poured himself a glass almost full of whiskey, clinking and clanging the bottle and the glass together loud enough to scare the birds away, and then lifted the glass in the air and said, "Here's to old sweethearts."

He wasn't looking at either me or Miss Amy when he said it, but I could tell from the look on her face that it upset her. It wasn't right for a married man to be toasting his old sweethearts right in front of his wife. Maybe I was just looking for things not to like about him, but I think anyone would agree that this wasn't a nice thing to say.

"Why don't we go in to dinner?" Amy said. "We've got a big roast, and I'm anxious to see if Jory still has his old appetite."

"Oh, I'm sure Jory still has his old appetite," said Crutchfield, and once more a look of pain went over Miss Amy's face. I don't know why it would bother her to have him say something about how much I could eat. Maybe she had a stomach ache or something.

When we got to the dining room and I saw the white tablecloth and the heavy silver and the fancy glasses set in front of the plates, and the two Mexican women, Francisca and Luisa, who I knew from the old days and who gave me big smiles when our eyes meshed, it gave me a strange feeling, and without even thinking about it I went over to my old chair.

"Hey," said Crutchfield, "you don't want to wear those heavy guns while you're eating supper. Why don't you put them over there on the sideboard?"

I was almost reaching down to take the weight off me when that little shiver went through my belly again. It would be really something if Stark came in on the prod and my guns were sitting over there with the dessert. I took my guns off every noon and night when I ate at the Davises but that was friendly and this was Indian territory. But wearing your hat and your guns when you were a guest for dinner wasn't polite. I was caught like when you're straddling a fence and your feet slip off the bottom pole.

"Have to wear them," I said. "Town law."

"Town law?" said Crutchfield, his loud voice even

louder than usual. "What kind of town law says that a man has to wear his guns while sitting down to dinner?"

"This ain't for regular people," I told him. "This is just for sheriffs."

"That's ridiculous," he said. "Why would there be a law like that?"

"Because somebody killed the sheriff before me and somebody else crippled the one before him," I said, "and they want to keep me around for a while."

I wondered what the town council would say about the law I just made up out of whole cloth. Crutchfield was shaking his head like he had just heard the craziest thing in the world, and it could have been that he had. But I wasn't parting with those guns until somebody unstrapped them from my dead body.

"Ah, here's the roast," called out Miss Amy, louder than she usually talked. It was like we were up on a stage somewhere and trying to get through to the sleepiest drunk at the back of the saloon.

Everybody was quiet for the next couple of minutes while the girls got everything on the table: meat and potatoes, and boiled cabbage and carrots, and flat Mexican bread and something I couldn't make out except that it tasted pretty good. Crutchfield had finished his glass of whiskey and was opening a big bottle of wine while the food was being put on the table. He then cut me a slab of beef that covered my whole plate, and I had to put the potatoes and other things over half of the meat. I knew right off that he was trying to do me in, but I was hungry from the ride and it was later than I usually ate, so I wasn't worried about the chore ahead of me.

"I don't suppose you want any wine, Sheriff?" Crutchfield asked, and I just shook my head at him.

"I don't think I want any either tonight," said Miss Amy, and Crutchfield gave her a long look that was also less than friendly.

"I suppose I shouldn't get annoyed," he said, "because

it means that much more for me, but you two are definitely not the life of the party. From what Amy told me, Sheriff, I expected that having dinner with you was going to be one of the most joyous occasions of my life. Might as well have had the preacher to dinner.'' He poured himself a full glass of wine, drank it down in one long swallow and then filled his glass up again.

"I worked on a ranch where the preacher was a drinking man," I told him, "and he wasn't no fun to have dinner with."

Amy asked me what I did on the ranch, and I told her I was the foreman, and Crutchfield wanted to know how many cows we ran.

"Somewhere around a hundred thousand," I told him.

"How many?"

"Well, Mr. Kingman told me it was a hundred thousand, but they were scattered over so many ranges that it was hard for me to tell altogether. When we did a drive, though, it looked like they were going to go by forever."

"And you were the foreman?" asked Crutchfield, his voice as much as calling me a liar. I'd seen men called out for a lot less voice than he was giving me.

"Yep."

"Why did you leave there?" asked Miss Amy.

"It was time to move on," I said. "There were things I liked, but there were more things I didn't."

I was afraid she was going to ask me more, and I wondered how I would get around telling about Mr. Kingman's niece, Sapphira, and how I had to kill Haines, the head wrangler, and how Craggins had stolen the money box with the Chinese cook, but Amy stopped there and I let out a sigh because I didn't even want to think about all that, let alone talk about it.

We kept eating and Crutchfield kept pouring himself wine, and Miss Amy would ask me if I remembered this or that and some of the other things that happened when I had lived there. The more wine Crutchfield drank, the more it was like he wasn't even there with us, and I kept looking at him and thinking how much he looked like Mr. Barron had but how different he was in every way. This went right on through the cake and coffee until finally even Miss Amy was out of things to say. I had cleaned up everything on my plate, so most of the time I was just chewing, but I don't think Crutchfield even noticed that I'd handled all he'd given me.

After the coffee we went into the big room, where the fire was going nicely by this time, and Crutchfield poured himself a big glass of brandy and stood there drinking it while Miss Amy told me that the ranch the Germans had owned, the ones that had almost killed her and me when they had tried to move in on Mr. Barron, was still up for sale and they were thinking of buying it.

"Maybe you could be foreman if we do," said Crutchfield, looking at me with those glassy eyes that drunks have.

"No," I told him, "no more foremanning for me. I don't know what I'm going to be doing, but it ain't ever going to be a foreman again."

"Well," said Crutchfield, "it's getting late and I'm sure you want to be getting back to town agan."

"Oh," said Miss Amy, "it's much too dark out there without a moon. You better stay overnight, Jory, and go back in the morning."

I was just about to say that I could find my way in the dark and it wasn't good for a sheriff to be away from town too long when Crutchfield broke in.

"I'm sure the sheriff doesn't want to shirk his duties," he said. "And besides, I can have Stark and a couple of the men go part way with him to make sure he finds the trail."

My heart almost stopped beating. I could just see me out there in the pitch black with Stark and his boys everywhere around me. When I disappeared, they would say that I was just fine when they had left me on the road. What with the eating and Miss Amy chatting away, I had been almost fooled into thinking everything was going to be all right. Coming out here had been one of the dumbest things I had ever done in my life, and it looked like I was never going to get a chance to do anything dumber.

"That would be silly," said Miss Amy. "I'm sure the town can get along without the sheriff for the rest of the night. And in the morning we can give him a big breakfast and send him on his way. There are still a lot of things we haven't talked about."

I sure thought we'd talked about everything there was under the sun, but I wasn't going to argue at that moment.

"I'm sure the sheriff—" Crutchfield began, but I cut him right off.

"I'd be pleased to spend the night," I told them. "My deputy can handle anything that comes up, and I can get an early start and be there in time for my regular rounds."

"I've got Stark right outside," said Crutchfield, "and it wouldn't be any trouble at all."

"No, it's late," I said, "and I don't want to keep him up past his regular bedtime, because I'm sure he's going to need all his strength in the morning."

"But we can—" Crutchfield began when Amy cut him off again.

"There, then," she said, "it's all settled."

And ten minutes later there I was in my old room with one of Mr. Barron's nightshirts laid out on the bed for me. Crutchfield had looked at Amy like you look at a bug you might or might not squash with your fingers, but all he'd done is grunt when she led me up the stairs.

It felt strange to be back in that room with the soft bed and the bureau where I'd kept my shirts and extra pair of long johns. I sat there on the bed for a while just thinking about it until all of a sudden I heard Crutchfield yelling from down the hall, but when I put my ear to the door he stopped. I didn't like that man for many reasons, and he felt the same about me if he was going to turn me over to Stark for a ride into nowhere.

I put my hat on the bureau and lay back on the bed, clothes, guns and boots on. The sheriff didn't only wear his guns at the supper table in this house; he wore them right to bed. I got up and wedged one of the heavy chairs under the doorknob and then lay back down again. I intended to stay up the whole night and figure out what I was going to do to get out of there with life and limb the next morning. But me being me, I fell right asleep.

GIDEON'S WAY 107

me over Conchita. How she found out about what we were

★ 13 ★

I'd blown out the lamp because I didn't want anyone to bust into the room with me in the light and them in the dark. I had meant to get up and sit on the floor against the right-hand wall so nobody could bang through the door and center in on the bed, but even while I was thinking of it, I fell asleep. Todd Davis could have waltzed in there and put me away for good.

I don't know if it was all that beef I had crammed down or the second piece of pie, but I sure had dreams enough for the whole population of Barronville. They were all mixed up with both dead and live people like my pa and Jocko and Mr. Barron and Miss Amy and Miss Sapphira and even Conchita, who had taught me the ways of the flesh as I heard a minister preach in a town whose name I never learned. I didn't know what day of the week it was, but I was weary of riding and anxious to sit a spell. I didn't want to go to the saloon, so I stopped in at the church, where it turned out to be a Sunday and they were having services. The preacher was going on about sin and evil with spit flying in all directions, and before he got through I could have sworn that he was enjoying talking about it more than condemning it. But he was the one who had pointed out to me that what I had been enjoying with Conchita was "the ways of the flesh."

I hadn't seen Conchita when I had ridden in and was wondering all through dinner where she might be, but I didn't want to ask Miss Amy because she had got mad at me over Conchita. How she found out about what we were doing I never knew, but she couldn't do nothing about Conchita being in my dream. Dreams are private property. This one sure was because in it Conchita was unbuttoning my shirt and Miss Amy was taking off my boots, and my pa and Mr. Barron were standing there looking on, and I could tell by their faces that they were mighty unhappy about what was going to take place, and that's what woke me up.

I knew where I was right off, and thought maybe I'd heard something outside the door, but it was dead still when I listened hard. It was pitch black and I wondered how far off dawn might be as I slid off the bed and worked my way over to the wall on my knees. That was one time when a watch would have come in handy. I looked out the window but couldn't see no stars or nothing, so maybe it was the darkest just before the dawn. In any case, it was time to get out of there and ride back to town. It could be that Stark and his boys were there right now waiting outside the door to settle my hash, or were over in the barn sharing my horse's stall or were laying on the trail back to town so they could dry-gulch me far enough off so that nobody would hear it or ever know about it.

I walked on my knees back to the bed and felt around till I found my spurs and then stuffed one in each pocket. Their jingle-jangle would have been like church bells gonging out in the hallway. I thought about taking my boots off, too, but there's something weak feeling about not having no boots on. What I had to do was keep up on my toes in more ways than one.

Easing the door open, I stole out into the hall, where it seemed even darker than in the room. It was lucky I had lived there before and knew where everything was because they had all sorts of chairs and flowerpots all along that stretch. When I reached the stairway, I turned around and went down backward so I could set down on my toes instead of my heels. Good thing there was a banister there because I slipped twice and would have gone down with who knows what kind of a hell of a crash if I hadn't had that rail to hang on to.

It was a little brighter at the bottom of the stairs, and as I turned to go toward the front door there was a blur of white to the left side, and I pulled and had my fingers tightening on the triggers when I heard Miss Amy whisper, "Jory?"

She must have come out of the big room, where there was a little bit of light coming from what had to be what was left of the flames in the fireplace. It's a good thing I'm as quick at not shooting as I am at shooting because I was more nervous than I'd even let on to myself. Having supper at the Barron place was a good lesson to me. Jesus only had one slinger out to get him at his last supper. I was surrounded by them.

"Jory, is that you?" she asked again. Coming out of the big room, her eyes weren't quite fixed yet for the dark.

"Yes, ma'am," I told her. "It's me, all right."

"Where are you going?" she asked. "Are you thirsty? Did Luisa forget to fill the pitcher in your room?"

"No, ma'am," I said. "I have a lot to do in town and I thought I'd get an early start."

"It's four o'clock in the morning," she said. "I thought that at least you'd wait for first light. Have some breakfast. Are you hungry now?"

"No, ma'am."

"We didn't really have a chance to talk," she said. "I want to talk to you, Jory. Since my daddy died, I don't have anyone to talk to."

There was a little catch in her voice when she said that, and all of a sudden I felt two arms go around me in the dark, and there was Miss Amy sobbing into my chest loud enough to wake up anybody who was a light sleeper. I looked over to where the staircase was, and wondered what Crutchfield would do if he came down the stairs with a lamp in his hand. I really wanted to get on my way, but Miss Amy still had good strong arms and there wasn't no way I was going to get loose unless I pried her off real hard. I leaned my head down next to hers to try to muffle the noises she was making, and next thing I knew she was kissing me real hard, shoving her lips against mine so that I could feel her teeth behind them. The last time she had kissed me was when we were hiding in the shallow hole we dug while the Barron hands and the Muller bunch was shooting it out in the dark. We both thought we were going to die then, and God knows what would have happened between us if that wagon full of powder hadn't blown up and lifted me right off the ground with my pants half down and my pecker straight out.

Mr. Barron told me the next day that Amy wanted to marry up with me, and that's when I had ridden off thinking I would never see her again. But here we were at four o'clock in the morning kissing in her front hall, me a sheriff and her a married woman. If somebody had told me two years before that this was going to happen, I'd have figured they were chewing on locoweed.

I've got to admit that it felt real exciting to have her gnawing on me like that because she had the kind of looks that caught your attention and then held it for a while. She also felt good to hold, her warm skin so soft and smooth, and she smelled just great. But at the same time I was thinking she belonged to another man and how I would feel if I came down the stairs and found my wife hugging and kissing somebody else. I pushed back at her so we had a couple of inches between us.

"Mr. Crutchfield a light sleeper?" I asked her.

She snorted. It was a strange sound, especially coming from Miss Amy, but it had to be nothing more than a good, old-fashioned snort, the kind Mrs. Jordan would make when Mr. Jordan said something she considered foolish.

"With what he drinks every night," said Miss Amy, "you could shoot a cannon off in the room without waking him up. It's the same every time. He uses me and then he rolls over and starts snoring loud enough to shake the pictures off the walls."

Uses me.

It took me a few seconds to get the drift, and then I could feel the blood rush to my face so fast that it was like my skin had caught on fire.

Uses me.

He was her husband and had every right to do what he wanted with her, but when I pictured it in my mind, it made me feel all crazy. It made me think of killing, which mixed me up because I'd had my chance to marry up with her and had ridden off. What right had I to think of killing somebody just because he was doing what married people did. But it was there; I felt it.

I pulled her in close again, and this time it was me that kissed her so hard that she gave a little "oof" sound from me squeezing so hard. I don't know what we would have done next if a gust of wind hadn't sucked air from the fireplace in the big room and made the coals glow bright for a few seconds. The light made me realize what the hell was going on in this front hallway and how I'd better be on my way before I got both of us killed.

I pushed back again and said, "I have to go, Miss Amy. There's been trouble between me and the Barron hands, and I would be better-off to get back to town."

"What kind of trouble?"

"Just barroom trouble," I told her, "but there ain't no love lost between me and Stark and some of your pokes."

"Nobody said anything. Jasper can't know about it either because he hasn't said anything. Stay for breakfast and we'll straighten it all out. We can't have our hands disturbing the peace in town."

"It'll all work out," I told her. "But now isn't the right time. I really have to get cracking. Thank you for the nice supper."

"Jory, I have to talk to you."

"Next time you're in town we—"

"No, I have to talk to you sooner than that. Meet me tomorrow at the pond where I used to go swimming. Meet me there at two o'clock."

Damn! I was going to have to buy me a watch after all.

"I don't know, Miss Amy. I have—"

"Jory, please. You must meet me. I have to talk to you."

"I'll be there," I told her. "But I really have to go now."

She tightened her grip a little like we were going to kiss again, but this time I pried her off hard enough to make her drop her arms. I went to the door and eased it open, slipped through and pulled it tight again. Moving quick as I could in the dark, I went down the stairs and headed for the horse barn. It was going to be no easy time over there because I didn't know which stall they had put Bones in, or whether they had let him run loose in one of the corrals. I had to try the barn first. If I didn't find him, then I might have to take one of their horses and trade off again some time in the future. That would be a pretty mess to bring about, but I didn't know no other way to get out of there with my scalp still on my head.

I was in such a hurry that I went right into the barn without thinking, and when the hand reached out to touch me, I was so startled that I didn't even think of going for my guns but just stood there like one of those carved Indian figures they have in front of stores sometimes.

"Mr. Jory?" a voice asked, and I knew right away it was Pedro.

I swallowed so my heart would go back down to its rightful place. "Pedro."

"I have your horse all saddled, Mr. Jory. I was not sure what you would do, but I wanted to be ready for whatever it was."

"You been here all night?"

He didn't answer, and I reached out and gave his arm a squeeze even harder than the one that Miss Amy had put on me. I would have been as glad right then to kiss him as I had been with Miss Amy.

"I thank you," I told him.

"*Por nada,*" he said. "We must walk out quietly until we get to the outer gate."

"I can find it myself."

"I will walk with you, *señor*."

He held the reins and I held on to the side of the saddle and it wasn't long before we were at the gate. I could have done it myself, but it probably would have taken double the time.

After I had swung up in the saddle, I reached down and put my hand on Pedro's shoulder. "If ever you need me," I told him, "I will be there."

"Help the *señora*, Mr. Jory," he said. "Her sadness is our sadness."

"I will do what I can," I told him, and put the big black into a slow walk even though he bounced like he was raring to go. I didn't want to make more noise than was necessary that close to the bunkhouse.

Light broke a short time after I was on the wagon trail, and it made me feel good and also very hungry. When I was sitting there in the dark in that bedroom, I hadn't been too sure I was ever going to eat again, but now that I knew I was, I was hungrier than ever, and I put the big black into a soft canter.

We hadn't gone more than a few miles when I spied a horseman coming toward me at full gallop. I loosened my right-hand gun a touch in the holster and tightened up on the reins a bit in case I had to make a sudden move of some kind. She was almost right on me before I realized that it was Andy riding hell for leather, and when she saw it was me, she reined up on her horse so hard that his front legs went right up in the air.

"You all right?" she yelled, looking down the road behind me.

"Sure I'm all right," I told her. "Why wouldn't I be all right?"

"Mrs. Davis came to my house before dawn and said you hadn't come home. She was worried your horse might have throwd you or that something had happened at the Barron place."

"How did she know I hadn't come home?" I asked her.

Her face went into all kinds of creases as she tried to puzzle that one out. "I don't know," she said. "Maybe she had stayed up waiting for you. What difference does it make?"

"So you come busting out here hell for leather, eh?" I said. "What was you going to do? Take on the whole Barron ranch?"

"I was going to do whatever had to be done," she said.

This time I could feel my face crease as I thought about that. This girl was going to ride into the Barron ranch all by herself against all those gunslingers just to save my bacon. Damned foolish, but it gave me such a good feeling that I thought my chest would bust.

Bacon. Damned I was hungry.

"Let's go back to town," I told her, "and have some breakfast. We can't have both the sheriff and the deputy away at the same time. How did things go last night?"

"Nothing special," she said.

"I didn't have nothing special either," I told her. That was pretty close to a lie, but there wasn't no need to get her as upset as I had been. Damn, but I never knew that being scared could make you so hungry.

SHORT STORY

chance that this always happened. There just to be some
one that was along. A leader of some opposite type
seared away that sort. It was one or the other. You
see a man . . .

★ 14 ★

We didn't talk again until we were on the edge of town,
me being preoccupied, as my pa used to say, with what
had happened at the ranch and how I had agreed to meet
Miss Amy at the East Pond that afternoon, and Andy
because she just didn't speak up unless she needed you to
pass the salt. Even then you had to figure she ate her beans
unseasoned a lot of the time.

There was no doubt that Miss Amy was one unhappy
lady and that Crutchfield was the one causing it. It was
amazing how a man who looked so much like her daddy
could be so different. Why the hell had she married up
with him in the first place? There was women who run out
on their husbands, sometimes because he was a drunk or
beat up on her or maybe because some drummer sweet-
talked her into believing that he was taking her to his home
town at the end of the rainbow. But Miss Amy wasn't no
ordinary woman and she couldn't run off and leave her
whole ranch behind. What it had ought to be was that she
could throw Crutchfield off the place if he was the one
causing her the grief. There ought to be a law like that
someday, and I'd like to be the sheriff that saw it carried
out.

But the way it was now, I didn't see what I could do to
help her out of her fix, short of shooting the man. That
was the second time I had thought about that, and it made
me feel twice as bad as the first time. The guns always
turned out to be my answer to everything. It wasn't by

chance that this always happened. There had to be something in me that was wrong somewhere, either in my head or in my soul, even though my pa said there was no such thing—the soul, not the head. Here he'd been dead more than three years now, and everything he had ever told me was clearer than it had ever been. I could even hear his voice saying it, but now there was no drunk sound in it, just the words in that clean, sharp, songlike way he spoke when he was sober. I wished I could of spent more time with my pa, but that had been cut off sharp by the tip of Ab Evans' boot. Nobody was ever going to take no boot to me, no matter how big he was. I reached down both hands and slid my guns just enough to have that special feeling go up my arms into the shoulders and then the head. Nobody. Nobody was ever going to take a boot to nobody as long as I was able to stop it.

When we reached the first house, I turned to Andy and said, "Why don't you come with me to Mrs. Davis'? I'm sure she'll be happy to give us both breakfast and then she'll know everything is all right."

"There's a prisoner in the lockup," she said.

It took me a bit to understand what she was saying, and even then I asked a dumb question. "What do you mean there's a prisoner in the lockup?" I said.

"Had to put him in there last night."

"We've never had a prisoner in there before," I told her. "Why would you put anybody in there?"

"He was disturbing the peace and paying no mind to the orders of a deputy sheriff," she said.

"Did you leave him some water?" I asked. "We gonna have to give him food? How long you going to keep him there? You know we ain't got no judges yet."

"I thought that would be something for the sheriff to decide."

That stopped me. She had done her duty as she saw it and had thought it necessary to put some poke in jail because he was carrying on, and here I was giving her grief about it.

"He do anything real bad?" I asked.

She thought about that for a short time. "Nothing too bad," she said. "He was drunk, that was for sure, and he was on the prod, that was for sure, and he wasn't going to listen to anybody, that was for real sure."

"How'd you get him over to the jail?"

"Four of the boys carried him over there."

I was happy that so many people had helped her in her time of trouble. There was plenty of men who would have just stood by and thought it funny to see any lawman, male or female, go up against a mean drunk.

"Let's stop by there first and see how he's doing," I told her, and that's what we did.

The smell in that room was so bad when I opened the door that my nose closed down of its own accord. Gawd knows what that man had done in his pants and he'd puked himself as well. He was big, that was for real sure. Big and mean-looking, with one of those beards that ain't neither here nor there, and just makes a man look dirty. He was laying on the bare floor because there wasn't nothing in that barred section to sit or sleep on, and she hadn't left him no water in a bucket or otherwise. You can't leave a person without water ever. Anybody who's ever been without water and maybe a chance of never getting none knows that. From now on that was going to be the rule no matter how bad the prisoner was who had to sit behind those bars.

The man heaved himself to his feet and stared at us, his eyes red like fire and his tongue all white when he opened his mouth to talk. "You gonna let me out of here?" he asked.

"That all depends on you," I told him. "We can't have people carrying on in this town just like they was animals. What outfit you with?"

"I just got paid off by Hackman," he said, "and was about to move through."

The whole left side of his face was purple and black and puffy like he had some wild disease that nobody had ever heard of. I'd seen bruises before but never one like this. When he passed out, he must have hit the floor like he was one of those bank safes.

"Well," I told him, wanting to get that stink out of the room as quick as I could, "I'm going to let you go this time, but I never want to see your face in this town again."

Andy handed me the keys off the wall and I unlocked the gate. The man had never looked at her once since we had come into the room, keeping his eyes on me like I was the Jehovah come to bring him resurrection. I stepped back so that I had drawing room in case he had any crazy ideas.

"What about my gun?" he asked as he stepped into the room.

"You don't own a gun in this town," I told him. "You're lucky if you've got a horse to ride out on."

"You can't leave a man without a gun," he said.

"Well, I guess you're going to be living or dead proof that you can," I told him. "Now get your stink out of here."

He moved fast enough then and was out of sight pretty quick.

"Let's leave this door open for a while," I told Andy. "There ain't nothing here for anybody to steal, and later on we'll throw some buckets of water on the floor. We may even have to dump some manure in there to try to sweeten it up a bit. Now let's go get some breakfast."

Mrs. Davis came running out the door even before we got down from our horses. She looked terrible instead of her usual neat and clean self.

"Thank God you're all right," she said. "I didn't know what had happened to you. Is there anything I can do?"

"Some breakfast," I told her. "We could use some breakfast."

The breakfast sure was good, but the pleasure was spoiled a bit by the way Mrs. Davis kept babbling on about how worried she had been and didn't know what to do and didn't want to leave Todd alone while she went looking for somebody but didn't want to wake him up and carry him around either, and she just went crazy until dawn came and she went looking for Andy. It wasn't like her at all, and I couldn't understand what had got into her. Living with her had been most pleasant up to then, but I wondered what it would be like to be married up with a woman who carried on so when things didn't go according to the usual way. I was a big boy; she didn't have to worry none about me.

I just kept eating and nodding at her, and Andy just kept eating, hardly ever looking up from her plate. If I was ever to get hitched, I think I'd prefer the Andy type of female rather than the Davis one. I suddenly realized that I hadn't been thinking in terms of female of late where Andy was concerned. Gawd! Wouldn't that be something if it came to pass that females started doing all the things men did and nobody thought twice about it? Then maybe men would have to start . . . I figured that I was still spooked from what had happened at the Barron ranch and not getting enough sleep. I cut another thick slice of bread and poured some molasses on it.

Andy thanked Mrs. Davis for the breakfast, said she had some business to attend to and took off. She carried the shotgun like it was part of her body and I went to the front window and watched her go down the street. She had been as worried about me as Mrs. Davis had been, but she didn't go carrying on like Injuns trying to coax some water out of the sky.

Mrs. Davis told me she thought I should take a nap, but I told her I had my rounds to do and didn't feel sleepy anyway. I had promised to meet Miss Amy at the pond, which would mean leaving town again, and it wasn't right that I should be going off two days in a row and leaving everything for Andy to handle. So I had best work twice as hard in the morning so's I wouldn't feel so bad about taking off the afternoon. I told her I might be real late for supper because there were some things I had to take care of, so she should just leave me out something easy in case she wanted to go to bed.

"I'll wait up until you get back," she said.

I could feel the red moving up to my face and I almost said something about not needing no mama at my age, but she looked so tired that I just told her not to worry about me and went out. I wondered if maybe I should look for someplace else to live, what with her worrying so much because of what happened to her husband. But then I thought about her cooking and how nice she washed my clothes and what a good feeling it gave me to sit at the table with her and Todd, that I didn't hold that thought for long. I guess I would have to admit that it was the cooking that was her hole card as far as I was concerned.

Roy was sitting at a corner table in his saloon writing down all kinds of figures on three sheets of paper spread in front of him.

"Well," he said, "here comes the big sheriff now that all the trouble's over."

"What trouble might that be?" I asked, pulling out a chair, turning it around so that I could keep an eye on the doors, and folding my arms on the back.

"What trouble?" he snorted, almost as good as a horse might have done. "You talked to your deputy today?"

"Just left her," I said.

"And she didn't say nothing about no trouble in here last night?"

"She had a galoot in the jail this morning," I said, "and told me he caused some trouble, but she didn't say anything about it happening here."

"Where is that galoot now?"

"I told him to get out of town and never come back."

"Did you see him go?" he asked.

"No, I didn't see him go. I told him what I'd do if I caught him around here again."

"Where's Andy?"

"I don't rightly know. She said she had some business

to attend to, and then I guess she'll be making her rounds, just like me.''

Roy stood up and limped around the table twice, his wrinkled face wrinkled up even more than usual. ''You better make sure she's all right,'' he said, ''because a man who was shamed the way he was last night might do anything to even the score.''

''I don't know what you're talking about,'' I told him.

''Last night. The thing that happened here last night.''

''What happened here last night?''

''She didn't tell you nothing?'' he asked again, his voice a mite higher than usual.

''I already told you that,'' I said. ''She told me there was a bit of trouble here, but four men helped her and it wasn't no big deal.''

''It's true that four men carried that son of a coyote over to the jail,'' he said, ''but that was all the help she got.'' He stopped and thought about it for a second. ''And when you get right down to it,'' he said, ''that was all the help she really needed.''

This time it was my turn to stand up and walk around the table.

''What the hell happened?'' I asked him, and this time I heard my own voice getting a little shrill. I wondered if what Mrs. Davis had was catching.

''Set,'' he ordered, and good mutt that I was, I did just that.

''He came in early,'' said Roy, ''and seemed to have a pocket full of money. He'd probably been to one or two other places before he come here, but he drunk enough at this stop to knock out two regular people. He was getting louder and louder and trying to slip his hands under the girls' dresses, both top and bottom, and I told him that if he wanted that kind of thing he should go over to the Paris, and he told me if I didn't shut up, he would put his hand inside my dress and turn me into a woman. I let that go because he was just standing at the bar then, and he'd bought a couple of rounds for two men I had never seen before neither, so I figured he'd be out of money soon after that or he'd go off to one of the other places.

"But then he took one of the girls out on the dance floor, and I noticed that he wasn't dancing with her, he was squeezing her until she couldn't breathe no more. And then he'd let her go for a bit, and then he'd squeeze her again. And every time she tried to yell out or call for help or whatever the hell she was trying to do, he would put the squeeze on her again, and I was worried that he might make a mistake and kill her. Everybody was watching by this time, but nobody did nothing about it, so I grabbed my club and started to come out from behind the bar, but the two pokes he'd bought the drinks for took the club away and held me so that I couldn't move. Damned gimpy leg takes away from my balance so I can't hardly do nothing if I can't stand straight. I started yelling at him to let her go, and that's when Andy walked through the doors."

"And nobody else was doing nothing?" I asked.

"There was a few of the regulars who looked like they might have wanted to," he said, "but there was also a lot of men laughing and getting a kick out of what the big fellow was doing, so nobody did nothing."

"What did Andy do?"

"She walked right up to where he was standing in the middle of the floor and she told him to let Millie go. He looked at her for a few seconds like he couldn't believe what was happening, and then he laughed and told her to go away before he did the same to her. She told him to let the girl go or she would put him under arrest. This made him laugh like hell and he threw the girl to the side and said, 'Come on and arrest me, Sheriff.' And Andy brought her shotgun in front of her, and he said, 'I'm going to take your toy away, Sheriff, and stick it up one of your holes.' And he made a move to grab the gun and she brought it up as hard and fast as I've ever seen anything move and caught him with the butt on the side of the face, and he went down like there wasn't going to be no tomorrow. I thought she'd killed him, and so did everybody else. The two men holding me let go, and I ran back behind the bar and got my own shotgun and came out to be beside her. She was standing there looking down at him like there was a pile of manure that she didn't feel like shoveling, and she hadn't shaded a hair, not a hair. I'd be proud to be a woman like that one there."

"And I just let that son of a bitch go," I said. "I should have gelded him."

"I think she gelded every man in the place," said Roy. "She pointed at four of them with her gun and told them to lift the carcass and haul it over to the jail, and they were right quick about it. She never came back, so I didn't know what happened after that. I would have gone looking for her, but one of the men told me she had locked the critter behind the bars, so I figured maybe she had gone home to bed. She'd sure done her day's work in those few minutes."

"How's the girl?" I asked.

"What girl?"

"The one who got squeezed?"

"Oh, Millie's all right, I guess. Wasn't nothing broken, just bruised up a bit. She's had just about everything else done to her, so this was just one more to add to the tally. Except he could have broken her back or killed her."

"I saw that man's face," I told Roy. "She works that gun better than anybody I ever saw, front end or butt."

"She's a wonder of the ages," said Roy. "She ought to be in a circus somewhere. Speaking of, where is she now?"

"That's what I aim to find out," I told him, and went looking for her. She was back at the jail trying to swab out the stink. I took the mop away from her even though she tried to hold on to it.

"I'll do this," I told her. "You've done enough for one day."

"People shouldn't see the sheriff doing woman's work," she said. "Then they won't have respect."

"They won't do that," I told her, "because then they might have to deal with you. Why didn't you tell me what happened at Roy's saloon last night?"

"I did," she said.

"You didn't say nothing about the squeezing and you going up alone against that *hombre*."

"Wasn't no need to."

"Well, from now on, I want to know everything that happens," I told her.

She didn't answer.

"There," I said, wringing out the mop with my bare hands and throwing the bucket of water out into the street.

She grabbed the mop away and showed me how to squeeze it dry without touching it.

"That way you don't get no puke on your hands," she said.

"I'm learning," I told her. "I'm learning."

"I did the whole town," she said. "Everything's quiet."

"I have to go out this afternoon," I told her. "Probably won't be back until after supper."

She just looked at me, her face set like a top gambler.

"I have to see somebody," I said, "and I don't know exactly when I'll be back." I don't know why I kept repeating myself to her, or didn't tell her where I was going and who I was seeing. She just kept looking at me with that stone face. I had the crazy feeling she knew where I was going and who I was seeing, but all she did was look.

"You think you can handle . . ." I started to say, and then stopped myself cold. She was the one who had ought to ask me that question. God help anybody who tried to put the squeeze on this town while Andy Colvin was riding shotgun.

★ 15 ★

The horse ain't the smartest animal in the world, but he gets to know you as well as you get to know him. Which maybe means that man ain't that smart neither. The way Bones kept jigging to the side for no reason and stumbling when there wasn't nothing to stumble over made me realize that he sensed how troubled I was about meeting Miss Amy at the pond.

It wasn't that there was nothing wrong about two old friends getting together to talk over the problems that one of them had. Hell, her daddy would have backed me to the hilt if I had asked him for help, and it was only right that I should be doing the same for his daughter. But meeting her at the pond was a mite unsettling because that was where we were jumped by the three Muller men when Miss Amy was swimming with no clothes on. I still wondered if I killed them because they were going to do us in, or whether it was mainly because they had seen Miss Amy's naked body. She had been so scared that she had pressed that very same body against me when it was over, and strange as it may sound, I could now at this very moment, two whole years later, still feel what it was like with her pushing into me, and how she had smelled so clean and fresh from the pond, and the wild things that had gone through my head while we were squeezing each other.

Here I was eighteen years old and Conchita was the only woman I had ever done it with. Most of the men I had come across in the two years I was on the trail had talked like they did it every day and with a different woman each time. And sometimes they would look at me and say, "What about you kid?" And I would smile and try to look like I done it twice a day with every female that crossed my path. I knew if I told them that Conchita was the only one they would hoot and holler and go around telling everybody what a tenderfoot I was. Only I guess that wouldn't be quite the right word. Tender something-or-other part of your body would be better.

To tell the truth, in all my wandering I hadn't really seen nobody who had made me nervous in that special way. There were lots of dance-hall girls and women in bars, but mostly they were ugly enough to make a rabbit think twice. Good-looking women like Miss Amy and, yes, Mrs. Davis never came into my life except to see a few in a store or walking down the street with their mamas. Gawd, I wondered what it would be like to go to bed every night with someone like Miss Amy, and, yes, even Mrs. Davis. I wondered if Mrs. Davis would talk as much in bed as she had at breakfast that morning. What I would like would be a cross between Miss Amy and Mrs. Davis and toss in a bit of Andy to quiet things down and have you a woman who would back you like she was a man. That would be something to have a wife like Andy because she was, after all, a woman, and she had all the rights and privileges that Miss Amy and Mrs. Davis had. I laughed out loud at the thought of it, and Bones stopped dead in his tracks, turned his head almost three-quarters of the way around, and looked at me like I was plumb out of my mind. Which could of been a case where the horse was smarter than the man.

I started to recognize places where Miss Amy and I had ridden when I was bodyguarding her, and the closer we got the more jumpy I became. I had started out early so I would be sure not to be late, but as I looked up at the sun, I figured it couldn't be more than one o'clock, and I wished I'd taken some bread and meat along so I could have sat me down in the shade somewhere and used the extra time to quiet down my belly. It was going to be forever until suppertime, and I was probably going to be late for that. The best thing would be to find me a place and gnaw on twigs until Miss Amy got there.

Except that she was already there when I rode up. Her horse was tied to the branch of the tree she was sitting under, and she was leaning back against the trunk with her hat off and her eyes closed. Damn, but she looked pretty. Beautiful. She had to be about twenty-five years old, according to what her daddy had said two years before, but she hadn't yet lost none of her looks. Sometimes I would be amazed at how quick a woman turned wrinkled and old-looking, especially when they lived on a ranch.

I don't know how long she'd had them open again, but when I got through sizing up the rest of her and returned to the face, there were those big brown eyes gazing at me kind of strangelike. It was almost like she had been doing the same thing to me that I had been doing to her. Except that girls couldn't ever think like that.

She pulled a big gold watch out of the pocket of her jacket and said, "You're early." When she saw me looking at the watch, she said, "This was my daddy's. Jasper said he wanted it, but I like to carry it around. It's like my daddy was still ticking along with me."

"That's a mighty handsome watch," I said, getting off my horse and tying him down.

"I want you to have it," she said, suddenlike, holding it out toward me. It took me a bit to think and then talk.

"I couldn't do that, Miss Amy," I said. "Your daddy would want that to stay in the family, and someday you'll give it to your son, and he'll be proud to carry it."

She put it quick back in her pocket, like she'd had serious second thoughts about what she had done.

"I don't want to have a son," she said. "I don't want to have any children with Jasper Crutchfield."

I didn't know what to say to something like that, so I sat down in front of her and crossed my legs just like an

Indian. If I'd of had a blanket, I probably would have wrapped it around my shoulders in the way they do when they're squatting somewhere in town.

"Jory," said Miss Amy, putting her hand on my knee, and I could feel the warmth right through my thick wool pants, "I am caught in a trap and don't know how to get out of it. I don't know that I can get out of it. Jasper has taken over my daddy's ranch, and I no longer have any friends or people around me I can trust except for the Mexicans."

"You've got friends in the valleys all around here," I told her. "Invite them over or go visit them."

"I tried," she said, "but nobody will come anymore. Darcy Fallon even told me in town that her father suspected that the beef he was missing might be in the Barron herd. I asked Jasper about that and he went into a rage that lasted all day. And he won't let me go anywhere. He says he needs me around all the time. It's like I was a prisoner, but I don't know what I've done wrong."

"You haven't done anything wrong, Miss Amy," I said, almost putting out my hand to her knee, but she still had hers on mine, and I figured two knees was a bit too much with a married woman.

"You've got to help me, Jory," she said. "If you hadn't run away, we would have been married and none of this would have happened."

Gawdamighty, isn't that just like a woman. Here she was blaming the whole thing on me, and I hadn't done one blessed thing wrong as far as I could see. I was sorry now that I hadn't married up with her because all I'd been thinking about since she'd kissed me in the dark hallway was what it would be like to be doing stuff like that all the time. I'd tried to fool myself by not thinking about it on the ride out, but I hadn't even fooled the fool horse. I racked my brain to think of something to say in my defense, but nothing came to mind. Maybe I didn't have no defense.

"Things are getting worse and worse," she said, "and this morning he acted crazy when he talked about you."

"He didn't see us in the hallway, did he?" I asked her.

"What?"

"He didn't see us kissing in the hallway last night, did he?"

"He was drunk as a coot," she said, "and besides, I kissed you before I ever kissed him."

That was another one that puzzled me. Was I the first boy she ever kissed, and did that give me some kind of permanent rights? I wished my father had been given more time to teach me about the law. There was so much to learn and time was passing me by.

"Miss Amy," I said, "I don't know what I can do to help you. You're married up with him all legal and square, ain't you?"

She nodded and I could see her eyes getting all wet, and I wanted to take her in my arms and kiss her eyes dry again. She was right. It was all my fault to begin with. If I hadn't ridden off, we would be married now, and there wouldn't be any Crutchfield and I would be wearing her daddy's watch and running the ranch all fair and square with no neighbors wondering if any of their beef was on our land. But I hadn't been ready to take on what Mr. Barron kept calling "responsibility," and I had to go out on the trail to find out. Being foreman for Mr. Kingman had shown me I could run a big spread even if I didn't know nothing about it, and being sheriff had showed me I could handle "responsibility" even though I didn't know much more about that than when I rode back into town.

So there we were sitting under that tree with Miss Amy trying to keep from crying while she was rubbing me harder than ever on the knee, and me wanting to take her in my arms and kiss her some more and maybe even . . . And that's how they got the drop on me. I suppose in the condition I was in I wouldn't have heard a stampede coming even while cows were stomping me, but it was still mighty mortifying to have the likes of them able to

sneak up and stick their guns in my face. I was glad that
Andy and Roy weren't there to see it.

There were two of them, and I recognized one from the
trouble in the Paris France Saloon, but the other, a tall,
skinny cuss, was new to me.

"Howdy, ma'am," said the skinny one. "It's a good
thing we happened along to keep this man from hurting
you any more than he already has."

"He hasn't hurt me at all," said Miss Amy, jumping to
her feet, and while she was doing it, I slowly stood up at
the same time.

They both had their guns pointing straight at me with
their fingers fairly tight on the triggers, and they were
close enough so that even Todd Davis couldn't have missed.
What worried me most, though, was that Miss Amy was
standing so close, so I eased myself back a few inches at a
time while she was yelling at them.

"This is an old friend of mine," she hollered, "and he
even had dinner at our house last night. Mr. Crutchfield
will be mighty angry when he finds out how you treated a
friend of ours."

"Well, now, missy," said the other one, "that ain't
exactly the way we heard it. Just this morning, Mr.
Crutchfield and Stark was talking, and they was saying as
how the sheriff was too big for his britches and maybe
needed to be taught a lesson. And now we find him in the
woods here with you. Ain't nobody going to find fault
about a man getting killed for messing with another man's
wife."

Did you ever have that feeling where something is
happening to you and you would swear that it had happened before? Like you had dreamed it or something, and
then it came true? Except that it had really happened to me
and Miss Amy. This was where the three Muller men had
jumped us when she was swimming without any clothes
on, and I had to shoot all three of them before they killed
us, and I finished off the one who was only hurt because
he had seen Miss Amy's naked body, and I didn't want

anybody in the world to go around talking about that. Now here were these two about to kill me or take me back to the ranch, and God knows what they would do to me there, but the main thing was that they would tell Crutchfield and maybe everybody else how I was sitting in the woods with Miss Amy while she was rubbing my leg.

I pulled and shot each one of them square in the right shoulder, which knocked both of them to the ground, where they lay yelling and thrashing about. I watched real careful in case one of them tried to grab his gun with his good hand, but that seemed to be the last thing they had in mind. I picked up both guns off the ground and laid them off to the side where they would be out of the way until I collected them again.

Miss Amy was standing there with her right fist stuck in her mouth, her eyes seeming as round as silver dollars, and little sounds coming out of her. I suppose a woman does get surprised when two guns blast off when she's not expecting them, but then again, a gun hardly ever goes off when you are expecting it. These two galoots had felt so big and mighty because they had guns on me, and they were as surprised as Miss Amy when the bullets tore into them. It's hard to figure a man. All they had to do was squeeze those triggers a little harder when they saw me go into the draw and I would be the one laying on the ground moaning or forever quiet. But there are some as come to the guns natural, as Jocko always told me I did, and there are the rest who think they are gunmen but don't really have what it takes.

To tell the truth, I was feeling pretty good about what had happened even if it didn't pleasure me to see two men rolling and groaning on the ground. Both shots had gone exactly where I had wanted them to, and that was after a long time without the guns and only that one practice session with Andy. I had been unsure about whether I still had what it took, but now I knew I really had the feel again.

One of the men, the skinny one, was bleeding pretty

bad, and Miss Amy was kneeling down beside him, pushing in with her hand to try and slow it down. I took his kerchief and rolled it into a ball and then tied it down with his gun belt. It kept slipping if you didn't hold on to it, but it was the best I could do.

"I've got to get these men back to the ranch so they can be looked after," said Miss Amy.

"I'll take them back to town," I told her.

"But the house is only an hour away and it's two hours back to town. Juanita Méndez is very good with gun wounds."

"I have to take them back to town, Miss Amy," I told her. "The barber's supposed to be pretty good with gun wounds, too."

"Jory, that's crazy," she said. "I know you can't go to the ranch, but if you'll help me get them on their horses, I can lead them back."

"No, Miss Amy," I said, "they're under arrest for pulling a gun on the sheriff, and I'm going to take them back to town and put them in jail."

"Jory . . ." she began, but I took her by the arm and pulled her off to the side.

"Miss Amy," I said, "you don't want these two going back to the ranch and telling your husband that we were out here together. You'd be in a heap of trouble and maybe this time you'd end up with more than a bruise on your face."

Her hand went right up to the spot where you could barely make out that the color wasn't quite right, and she stared at me for a couple of seconds. "But we can't . . ." she began again.

"Yes, we can," I told her. "I'll see that they get to town and their wounds are looked after, and then I'll see to it that they leave town as soon as they are able. Meanwhile, I'll try to figure out what we can do about your problem because right now I haven't even an idea on where to start on it. We need time. Now go wash your hands off in the pond and skedaddle back to the ranch in case they're wondering where you are. The quicker you do that, the quicker I'll be able to get these two to the barber."

She gave me another long look and then went through the bushes to where the pond was. She was back mighty quick, gave me another look, and then rode off without saying a word. Things were getting mighty complicated.

It took me a while to get those two fixed on their horses so they wouldn't fall off, and then I put their guns in my saddlebag and started back to town. It took us three hours to get there because every time I tried to speed up a bit one or the other of them would fall off his horse even though I'd tied them on pretty good.

I took them straight to the barbershop and told Mr. Crumpet to fix them up as best he could. He said he'd do as good as he knew how. Then I went over to the jail, where Andy was sitting on one of the chairs, and told her to go over to the store and get some blankets and a pot for drinking water and a pail for when they had to get rid of the water and a couple of plates and a couple of spoons and charge them to the town.

She hadn't been gone five minutes before Mr. Kraft came busting in to find out "what the hell was going on."

I told him I had two wounded prisoners and they would need a place to sleep and eat until they was well enough to leave town. He wanted to know how come I had two wounded prisoners, and I told him I had gone out to check on the cattle that had been reported missing and these two had come along and pulled a gun on me.

"They're Barron people, aren't they?" he asked.

I told him that we hadn't discussed it but that I figured they were because I recognized one who had been in the fracas over at the Paris France Saloon.

"Sometimes I get the feeling you're making things worse instead of better," he said, but he left to give Andy the things I had asked for.

So there we were that night with two sick prisoners laying on the floor in the barred section, groaning away

like they was full of bullets instead of having just one each
go through them. I'd bought a pot of soup from Mrs.
Fraker, and we'd spooned some down them as best we
could, but they weren't that interested in eating. I sure was
because it was near eight o'clock and I hadn't taken either
the noon meal or supper, so we locked the door and Andy
went to make a turn around the town to see that everything
was all right.

Mrs. Davis was waiting for me with a meal she'd kept
warm on the back of the stove, and I finished off all there
was and could have eaten more but didn't want to cause no
fuss.

Mrs. Davis was looking like herself again, all neat and
tidy, with her face shining like it had been given a good
scrubbing and her hair pulled back so that her eyes looked
bigger than usual. She didn't look at all like Miss Amy,
but she was real pretty in her own way. She mostly kept
quiet while she was getting the food and I was eating, but I
could see she was building herself up to something and I
wasn't going to be able to go to bed without answering at
least one question.

"Did you have a nice day?" she asked.

"Tolerable," I told her. "Just tolerable."

★ 16 ★

On my way to the jail the next morning, I saw Andy standing outside the town privy with the stock of her shotgun resting on her hip, and I figured one of the prisoners was well enough to have his body pushing things out again. I waved to her and she wiggled the barrel of the gun at me. People don't appreciate what a lawman has to do sometimes. There she was guarding stink and nobody would think twice about it.

One of the saddest-looking horses I ever did see was tied up to the post outside the jail. I don't mean that it was sick-looking or anything like that; it was just the way he was standing and the way he lifted his head slowly and looked at me when I walked up. I'm not sure if sad or mournful would be the right word. It was like this horse had seen things that would break the hardest heart in the world, and he could tell you stories that would make a grown man cry. That's crazy, I know, but I would defy anybody to look in this horse's eyes and not feel exactly the same way I did. It made me shake my head in wonder as I walked through the door.

What turned out to be another wonder was sitting in the chair by the table, his eyes fixed on the prisoner who was on the floor leaning against the back wall. I noticed that the pot had fresh water in it, and there was a plate of buttered bread on it, so I figured Andy had got there real early to take care of the prisoner chores.

The man in the chair was fairly little in size, couldn't

have been much more than five and a half feet tall, and he looked like he might of been fifty years old or even more. His face was burned almost black from the sun and the wrinkles were so deep that you could see white streaks at the bottom of them. There was a big gray mustache drooping down from over his lip, and though he must have heard me come in, he kept on staring at the prisoner like he was trying to memorize something from a book.

But the biggest surprise of all was when he finally turned toward me and I saw pinned on his shirt a badge that said U.S. MARSHAL. We all know that not just anybody becomes a federal marshal; he is appointed by the President of the United States his very own self. The President of the whole United States. I was sheriff of Barron County, but I hadn't ever been to one of the other towns I was supposed to be sheriff of, the nearest of which was fifty miles away, because the town council said I was only to worry about Barronville. This made me feel like I was shirking my duty a bit, but they had hired me and that's what they wanted me to do. So I really was only a town marshal, but my badge said sheriff.

Now a federal marshal, he covered the whole territory, and he could call out the United States Army to help him if he needed it. A man in a Dodge saloon once told me that federal marshals weren't so much, that they got their jobs from politics rather than worth, but I was pretty sure the President of the United States wouldn't appoint a man to a position like that if he wasn't some kind of top dog in just about everything.

But here was this little man sitting there looking at me like I was a horse he might be planning to buy, and it appeared like he might go on doing that all day if I didn't take some kind of action.

"Howdy," I said.

He thought about that for a minute, then stood up, walked over and stuck up his hand. I say stuck it up rather than out because I was quite a bit taller than he was. I took his hand and we shook twice before he dropped it down again. He was wearing one gun whose handle was pretty worn, and leaning on the wall in the corner was a Winchester rifle that I took to be his.

"My name,' he said, "is Tyrone Guthrie. Marshal Tyrone Guthrie."

"I'm Jory," I told him.

"I've been all over the territory," he said, "some places twice, but this morning I have witnessed the strangest sight that mortal man was ever taken aback with."

Guthrie talked in a kind of singsong that had you following along like when a whole bunch of people are singing in a saloon. It wasn't church-type singing; it was strictly saloon. It kind of kept you from talking because it would have been like interrupting a piece of music. No matter how bad it might be, you always waited for the end.

"I have encountered a young lady who tells me that she is a deputy sheriff of this county. Young man, there is no such thing. Women have their uses—many of them good or pleasurable, or both—but there is no way that a woman can be a law officer, deputy sheriff, or what you will. As soon as word of this gets out, people will start coming from hundreds of miles away to view this phenomenon and to dare her to arrest them, and blood will flow in your streets. I don't know who is responsible for this foolishness, but it must cease and desist as of this very moment."

"I'm the sheriff here," I told him. "You may be a federal marshal, but that don't give you any right to come in here and tell us how to run the town. I'd take this girl over almost any man I've ever known, and I'll thank you to state your business and then get on your way."

"That's clear and simple," he said, "and I will take your advice as offered. But remember that I have warned you of the consequences, and someday you will pay a bloody price for your not taking my wise counsel."

I waited him out. I didn't want to hear no more of this foolishness from this bandy runt who came in out of nowhere and tried to tell me how to run my business.

There wasn't no way I was going to let this man get me flustered.

"I am here," he said as he pulled a legal-looking paper out of his pocket, "to arrest and take into custody one Jasper L. Crutchfield."

He flustered me. I couldn't get no air. It was like somebody had punched me square in the belly when I wasn't expecting it, and I just stood there staring at him, my mouth open but nothing going in or out of it. I don't know what my face looked like, but I could see his eyes narrow a bit as he tried to figure out my problem.

It was at this moment that Andy came back with her prisoner, looked at the two of us standing there, and then put the man back behind the bars. She then went and leaned against the wall right next to the little man's Winchester.

I felt my stomach go out and the air come in again. "You are here to do what?" I asked. I had heard and understood what the man said, but it all seemed so impossible that I had to ask the question.

"I am here," he repeated, "to arrest and take into custody one Jasper L. Crutchfield."

"On what charges?"

"On the charges that he and parties unknown did embezzle fifteen thousand dollars from the United States Army."

"How'd they do that?"

"By filing false invoices on the purchase of cattle and pocketing the funds for their own use."

"Crutchfield did that?"

"The attorney general says he has indisputable proof that said Crutchfield did file false invoices on four separate occasions, defrauding both the army and the United States government."

Indisputable proof. I liked that and put it in my memory to use someday. I have indisputable proof that you are drunk and disorderly. I have indisputable proof that you did not pay your tax to the town. And now there was indisputable proof that Jasper L. Crutchfield, husband of Miss Amy Barron, was a crook and was going to jail. According to this little man. But he was a federal marshal, wasn't he? And federal marshals didn't just go around arresting people unless there is a reason. Gawdamighty! I told Miss Amy I would figure out something, and here it was. Well, I didn't exactly figure it out, but here it was anyway.

"Mr. Crutchfield," I said, "runs the biggest spread in this area. Why would he want to steal from the government?"

"The incidents took place when Captain Crutchfield was purchasing officer for the United States Army Commissary Department," said Guthrie, "and two members of that department, who have confessed and given evidence, were involved with him and parties unknown."

"What's all this 'parties unknown' business?" I asked.

"We are sure," he said, "that in addition to filing false invoices, the captain and the 'unknown parties' did divert cattle from herds headed for government pens and sell them on the open market. However, the only thing we can prove is as to the invoices, so we will have to interrogate Captain Crutchfield to find out who else was involved."

Interrogate. I wasn't ever going to question prisoners anymore; I was going to interrogate them.

"Do you have a plan for arresting and taking into custody Mr. Crutchfield?" I asked.

"I will go out to wherever the ranch is and do it," he said firmly, jutting his pointed chin up at me. "And I am asking you as sheriff to accompany me to show me the way and to assist if any assistance is needed."

"He's got about twenty hard cases working for him out there," I said, "and I wouldn't be surprised that some of them was your 'parties unknown.' However, I'm sure it is our duty to assist you in whatever you need, and the two of us will be happy to go along."

"Two of you? What two of you?"

"Me and Andy," I answered, pointing to her, standing against the wall.

"There is no way," he said, "that a U.S. marshal is going to take a girl along when he is making an arrest. I can just hear everybody in Austin if they found out that I took a girl along with me. I would have to resign my commission and go back into the furniture business."

Furniture business? Is that what you had to do to become a U.S. marshal? I began to wonder if that fellow in Dodge City was right when he told me that it was politics and not ability that got you appointed to the office. Of course, I was made a sheriff without having any experience, and I had made Andy a deputy without her having any experience, so it was possible that it was the same way with federal marshals. Only I didn't want to believe it.

"I don't care what they might say in Austin," I told him. "Those are gunslingers out there, and I ain't going anywhere near them without somebody to back me up."

"I'm going to be there with you," he said, raising up on his toes a little and pointing that chin at me again. "Or rather, you're going to be with me."

"Look," I said, "I know what she can do, and I trust her. On the other hand, I don't know nothing about you, and that means I can't depend on what you might or can do if it comes to a showdown. If she don't go, I don't go."

"I say who goes and who don't go," he said.

"You can say all you want, little man," I told him, "but saying ain't doing."

"It's your duty to assist me," he said.

"It's my duty to stay alive and not walk into any foolish situation. Either the deputy goes or none of us goes."

"Is there a mayor in this town I can talk to?" Guthrie asked.

"There ain't no mayor, but there's a town council," I told him, "and I been all through this thing with them already. They know what Andy can do and they know what I'd do if anybody tried to interfere with my official responsibilities.''

"So it's the two of you or nothing?" he said, and I could tell by his voice that he'd decided that two loaves were better than none.

"That's right."

"But I don't want to ride out of town with her, nor come back with her neither. She's going to have to meet us partway and then leave us when we come back."

I thought about that for a moment, looked over at Andy, who wiggled the barrel of her gun a bit, and said, "Well, we'll go along with that, but you should be ashamed to be acting like that in this day and age. Hell, man, it's 1871."

He didn't bother to answer, just went over and picked up his rifle, which was almost as tall as he was. I wasn't worried none about Andy, but I wondered how this little man would perform if things got hairy out at the Barron ranch.

I told him to wait a minute and walked over to the Emily Morgan, where I asked Roy if he'd take care of the prisoners until we got back some time before supper. He said he'd do that and didn't ask no questions. I almost stopped to tell him about Crutchfield, but then he might have wanted to go along, and I worried about him and his gimpy leg. It might have been smart to have deputized a posse, but there wasn't nobody in town who could really handle a gun, and I felt safer having just a couple of people who knew what they were doing rather than a bunch who might be running around doing more harm than good. Except that I didn't know how this furniture-business man might perform when the chips were on the table and Crutchfield and his boys were laying down their hand. I also didn't relish the thought of going back to that ranch, even though I did like the idea of putting Miss Amy's husband behind bars. Hot damn! But you couldn't fry no eggs without cracking the shells first. Maybe it was time to go out and crack a few shells.

So I sent Andy on ahead and there I was riding out on

the track to the Barron ranch with Marshal Guthrie. The combination of him and his horse wouldn't have put the fear in Todd Davis, and I hoped that he was better at his job than he looked. Which reminded me that I hadn't told Mrs. Davis I wouldn't be home for the noon meal, and I hoped that wouldn't put her into no fret again. I almost wished I was back on the trail, where I didn't have all these people pulling at me. It was that responsibility thing again; I had doubts that I was cut out for it.

We met up with Andy about three miles out, and Guthrie looked around as though he was afraid his Austin friends might be peeking at us. Hell, if anybody looked at the three of us riding there, they would have thought we were taking our daddy out for his exercise. I wondered what it was like to be old. And then I thought of Crutchfield and Stark and the rest of those gunslingers out there, and I wondered if I was ever going to get old.

★ 17 ★

We rode about an hour with nobody saying nothing to nobody, but if the old bugger was just waiting me out, he won the game.

"What's your plan?" I asked him.

He looked at me blank for a few seconds, like I'd been talking to him in Comanche.

"Plan for what?" he asked.

"How are you going to take Crutchfield out of there?" I said. "He's a pretty big man and he ain't going to come willing. And as I told you, he's got about twenty white punchers who don't much care for the law in town or out."

"That's all that's out there?" he asked, like twenty men with guns and willing to use them was nothing more than a horse swishing flies with his tail.

"There's about a hundred Mexicans," I said, "maybe twenty-five of them men, the rest women and kids, but they're all Miss Amy's hands, and I'm pretty sure they'll stay clear if trouble comes."

"Who's Miss Amy?" he wanted to know.

"It was her daddy's ranch," I told him. "She married up with Crutchfield after Mr. Barron died."

"Then she'll probably throw her Mexicans in with the white hands," said Guthrie. "A wife always sticks by her husband." He didn't seem worried none about going against either twenty hands or forty-five. I was beginning to won-der if maybe this little man was crazy, and that we were even crazier for going out there with him. What he didn't know was that I knew how Miss Amy felt about Crutchfield, and the main reason I was going along with all his foolishness was that I was ready to do anything to get Miss Amy out of her misery. I didn't know how long I could keep those two wounded critters penned up in jail before the town council wanted to know what was going on, and even if I took them far out of town before I let them loose, they could always double back and tell Crutchfield what they had seen by the pond. The only other thing was to kill them, and I knew for damn sure I couldn't do that. There had been a time when I would of put them down for good when they drew on me, but those days were over. A sheriff hadn't ought to kill nobody unless he has to. As a matter of fact, nobody should kill nobody unless he has to. People die soon enough without having anybody help them along.

"So what is your plan?" I asked again, like I was trying to get something through to Todd Davis.

"Well," he said, "I'll go up to him and tell him I've got a warrant for his arrest and take him into custody for transport to Austin."

"Just like that?"

"What do you mean just like that?"

"Do you think a grown man who is facing prison if he goes with you and who is a long way from any real law and who has enough gunslingers to blow a town away, let alone three lawmen all by theirselves, is just going to come along when you tell him to? If he doesn't try to kill us all and wait for the next marshal to come along, which could be some months from now, he might decide to take his people and go somewhere else, even to Mexico. I just don't think you've got a good plan there. I don't think you've got any plan at all. You ever done something like this before?"

"Well," he said after thinking about it for a minute, "I've been on the job for nearly two months now and mostly I've served papers on people in towns, but I'm ready to do my duty whatever it is and that includes what we're about to do now. Do you have a better plan?''

This was the first time he had asked a question in a civilized way, and for a second I almost felt sorry for the old coot. Here he had ridden God knew how many miles, and if things worked out, he'd have to ride them back with Crutchfield in tow, a man who would just have to sit on him once to squash him like a pancake. It wouldn't do Miss Amy any good if we was all to be killed trying to arrest Crutchfield. After that he might take her anywhere, and she'd be worse off than she ever was.

The problem was that I didn't have no idea either about how to grab the rattler behind the head and pull him out of the pit. One reason I've always had to be honest is that my mind can't work out no ''devious machinations,'' as my pa used to put it. He would rattle on about ''malefactors'' who would ''perpetually'' think up ''devious machinations'' that took advantage of honest citizens, and since I couldn't do none of these things, I knew in my heart that I would always be an honest citizen. I've had my temptations, that's for sure, but I never stepped across that line.

But here was a situation that required ''devious machinations'' of some type, and unless we came up with a pretty good one, we didn't have a hoot or a holler. We could skulk around the place in hopes of catching him unaware, but I doubted he ever traveled alone. And since one of the marvels of the big house was that they had indoor privies at the back, we couldn't even catch him with his pants down.

''You got any ideas about this, Andy?'' I asked her, and you could hear Guthrie snort like he had a chaw caught in his throat. I didn't hear nothing, so I looked around at her and she was shaking her head no. As she'd said to me once, I was the sheriff and it was my job to come up with the plan. Here I'd thought this little man had it all figured out and we would just have to back him up a bit, but now the baby was in my lap. And there was a good chance it was going to piss all over me.

We stopped to walk the horses a bit just before we topped the rise looking over the ranch, and then we sat while I thought a bit. I couldn't come up with nothing special, so I decided we had to take the bull by the horns.

"Maybe you had the right idea to begin with," I told Guthrie. "Why don't the three of us ride down as if we were just passing through and see what's going on? Just keep your warrant in your pocket until we need it. It could be we will get lucky and find Crutchfield by himself and waltz him out of there before anybody knows what's going on. If not, then maybe we will just tip our hats and ride out as if there was nothing special about our visit. Then we'll try to get some extra help, though I don't know nobody in town who would be good at this kind of thing, and come back and try it from a different angle."

"We can't do that," said Guthrie.

"Why not?"

"The girl can't ride down with us. We can't use a female to serve a federal warrant. It's against the law."

"First of all," I told him, "this here is my deputy, not just a female. Second, I want you to show me the law that says she can't help on a federal warrant."

"I don't carry the federal laws around with me," he sputtered, little specks of spit coming out of his mouth. "But I tell you it's the law and she can't come along with us. A judge would throw the case right out of court."

Now my pa had read me nearly all his law books and I'd read a lot of them myself, and I never come across a law that said such a thing. But then again, my pa's books weren't that new, and it could be that some new laws had been passed since the books was written. Someday I'm going to get enough schooling so that I can become a lawyer myself, and then I would know everything there is to know about such things. I didn't want to take any chances of having a judge throw the case against Crutchfield out of court because I had insisted that Andy come along with us, so I had to go along with what Guthrie was saying.

"Andy," I told her, "it might be good to have you up on the hill here with your rifle, and then if we have to skedaddle back, you can pepper up anybody who tries to chase us."

She gave me one of her looks, which said as much as words that she wasn't believing one word of what I was telling her, but then she nodded and got up to untie her horse. As we stood up to join her, I figured I better find something out now rather than when it might be too late.

"How fast are you with that gun?" I asked Guthrie.

"What?"

"You ever use that thing?" I asked, pointing to the beat-up six-gun in his holster. "How long does it take you to get it out?"

"To get what out?" he yelled, his eyes shifting to Andy for some reason.

"To get your gun out, Mr. U.S. Marshal," I said.

"I don't know. Whatever is needed."

"Show me," I said to him. "Show me how quick you are on the draw."

"I will not."

"You'll either do that," I told him, "or me and Andy turn right around here and head back to town, and you can pick up your prisoner by yourself."

"You're supposed to render me any aid I need," he said. "If you don't, I can have you brought up on charges, both of you."

"You ain't going to bring anybody up on charges if you're dead," I told him, "and you're probably going to be dead if you can't handle that gun at all. We ain't going anywhere with you until we know how far we can count on you to back us up if we need it. This ain't the furniture business, you know."

"All right," he said, "what do you want me to do?"

"When I say pull," I told him, "I want you to draw that gun as fast as you can. Don't point it at me because I don't want no accidents to happen. You turn and draw on the tree there."

He gave me a long look, blew out some air, and then turned toward the tree.

"Pull," I yelled, and then watched one of the sorriest sights I ever did see as far as guns were concerned. First of all, his hand didn't hit the butt right and he had to move it down to get a grip. Second, he had a hard time pulling the gun out of the holster because the leather was all dry and didn't want to let go. Third, he didn't clear the barrel all the way before he started to level it out and it caught on the edge of the holster and was almost torn out of his hand.

Finally, when he did get it out and pointed at the tree, the damned thing shook so much that I knew he'd have trouble hitting one of the cliff walls if he was stuck in a deep canyon.

"There," he said, turning around so that the gun was pointing directly at me, and I was pained to see that his finger was pressing on the trigger, "does that satisfy your goddamned impertinence?"

"Slow and easy," I told him in as soft a voice as I could manage. "You've got that gun pointing right at me and your finger's tight on the trigger. What I want you to do is take your finger off the trigger, turn a little bit so that you're not straight on to me, and then put the gun back in the holster."

He stared at me for a few seconds as if he didn't understand what I was saying, but then he did exactly as I told him. I could feel the wind drying the sweat on my forehead, and I turned to see that Andy had her shotgun dead on the little man. One more second and she might have blown him to bits right there, and I wonder what kind of soup you'd be in for killing a U.S. marshal. What I wanted to do was get on my horse and head back to town with Andy without having nothing more to do with this crazy little man. At first I had thought he was acting the way he did because of being brave at his job, but what it had to be was pure ignorance. He didn't have the slightest idea or the ability to be a lawman. I'd of bet the goddamned chairs he made fell apart the second time you sat on one of them.

But if we did turn around and let him go in alone, Crutchfield would eat him alive or at least bury him on the ranch where no one would ever find him again.

"What U.S. marshal?" they would say if anybody came out to inquire about his whereabouts. "We never saw no U.S. marshal."

It could be a couple of years before anybody got around to checking on him or trying to track him down, and by then the whole case against Crutchfield could also be lost in the shuffle. Then Miss Amy would be left in her fix and I wouldn't have done nothing to help her.

Nope. We had to go through with it one way or another, and it was going to be up to me and Andy to carry the weight of it. Not only would the little man be no help, but we would have to look out for him with whatever might be happening. Here I'd been so happy that Guthrie was going to solve all my problems for me when what he really did was add to them. On top of that, we weren't going to have no midday meal. I couldn't tell if the growling in my stomach was from that or because I had a bad feeling over what was about to happen. Well, whatever it was, we had best be getting to it.

We mounted up again and came to the top of the hill where we could look down on all the buildings. You could see Mexicans moving about but nobody else. The corral didn't look too full of horses, so I figured that maybe all or most of the white hands were on the range somewhere. They had to do something on the ranch besides carry guns and try to break up the town every Saturday night. Crutchfield could be out with them or in the house doing some paperwork.

"Andy," I said, "you get yourself behind that tree over there and get your rifle out. We're going to ride down and see what's what at the main house. If we can get the drop on Crutchfield, we'll put him in Mr. Guthrie's irons and bring him out. You watch the whole horizon while we're down there, and if you see a bunch of cowboys coming in from somewhere, you fire one shot to warn us and we'll ride up here as fast as we can. If there ain't no problems, you just cover us until we get back up here.''

She nodded at me twice, which was more than she usually said.

"Okay," I said to Guthrie, "let's mount up and see what's going on down there. I don't know how this thing is going to work, but there's only one way of finding out.''

As our horses picked their way down the hill, I slid both guns up and down a little in the holsters. They felt nice and easy and ready, but that didn't cheer me up like it usually did. I knew I could depend on the guns; it was luck I was worried about.

★ 18 ★

Going down that hill to the house was one of the longest trips I ever made in my life. I don't mean the distance we had to cover, because you could almost throw a rock from the top of the hill and maybe hit the porch of the big house. It was just that so many things were going through my mind that by the time we reached the front yard it was like it had taken days to get there. Well, maybe hours.

First of all, I've got to admit that I was a little bit scared. At least I think that funny feeling in my belly might have meant scared. I don't know exactly because it was a new feeling for me, one I'd never had. Part of the problem of getting older is that you start thinking a lot more about what can go wrong instead of just doing something and finding out about it later. I'd had funny feelings in my belly before, but it was almost always from eating too much or from not having enough to eat. This one was different, and I could feel the sweat puddling up under my arms, which had nothing to do with the heat of the day.

I tried to figure out exactly what was bothering me, and a lot of things came to mind. First of all, it was nothing but foolishness for me to come back to the Barron ranch, where there were all these people ready to do me in. Who'd ever have thought that this whole spread would be anything but a place where I'd be welcome and safe? I recollected all the good times I'd had there, and even those three days that the Germans had held me and Miss Amy prisoners didn't seem that bad when you looked back on it. It was the good that came through.

Part of my problem was the little man riding alongside me. If I'd had only my own neck to take care of, I am pretty sure I wouldn't have had this funny feeling in my belly. I knew what I could do and how to go about it, but I had no more idea what the marshal would do if things got hairy than if he was the man in the moon. Things are different when you have to worry about taking care of somebody else besides yourself. There was no doubt in my mind that if it came to a showdown, I would have been better off if Guthrie was on their side instead of mine and Andy's. But this way I had to worry about keeping him from getting killed or hurt, and that would spoil my concentration. When things are going wrong, you have to know everything that's happening in all directions and with all the people around you, those in front and those who might be anywhere. It isn't just your eyes that are important in a gunfight. Your whole body right down to your toes has to feel what's in the air. I guess maybe it's kind of like what they say about the way bats fly so fast at night. They have these things in their heads that tells them when to dodge, when to go up or down. Whenever I've been mixed up in something that came to people pulling guns, I've always had this little tingle that tells me if a fly has moved from one spot to another on the ceiling or if a man suddenly holds his breath as he goes into his draw. I can see it; I can hear it; I can smell it.

But having to worry about Guthrie was like having corks put in my nose and mouth and blinders on my eyes. I almost asked him to give me the papers and go back up the hill with Andy, but I realized that only a U.S. marshal could do it all legally and make the arrest. I wanted Crutchfield taken away so bad that I was willing to lay my life on the line to help do it. This was more than a case of performing my sworn duty; the law and Jory were after the same ends.

When we came to the hitching rack at the front of the house, I slid off Bones and looked around in all directions. It was quiet, too quiet. The Mexican kids were probably in the school that Mr. Barron had started on the ranch, and the women were doing their laundry down by the river or were cooking. You really couldn't see the barns or the Mexican houses from where we were. It was like being in the middle of nothing.

I didn't tie the horse to the rack, just let the reins hang over his head. Unless something spooked him real bad, he'd stay there until I mounted up or called him to come over. Guthrie didn't hitch his horse neither, but I doubt that you ever had to tie that sad-looking creature. He probably went to sleep the minute you stopped and didn't wake up until you gave him a boot.

I walked over to the porch stairs and listened again, but there wasn't no noise coming out of the house. It was too late for everybody to be still in bed and too early for a nap. It was almost like one of those ghost towns you go through on the trail sometimes. There are all these buildings with nobody human in them. Had Crutchfield heard that Guthrie was coming and moved everybody off the place?

I went up the stairs as soft as I could, but the marshal stubbed his toe on the very first step and came down on his knees with a thud. The front of his legs had banged against the second step awful hard, and he pushed himself up and limped around for a minute before starting up again. I was just as bad as he was because I was standing there gawking at him instead of staying ready in case somebody came busting out of the house or from around the corner. The two of us were good enough to be clowns in a circus.

I didn't know whether to knock on the door or not, but decided that it would be foolish to bang away and let them know we were there. So I turned the knob and the door opened easy enough, except for some loud squeaks. The hallway was empty, but I waited outside for a minute to see if anybody would come to find out what the squeaks were about. Nobody. It was getting kind of spooky.

Guthrie came in and started nosing around in a peculiar way. It suddenly came to me that he was checking out the furniture. It would have been funny if we weren't in the kind of pickle that could cost us our lives. I could feel the mad building in me, even though I knew it was of no matter. Let the old coot figure out how much the chairs and tables and mirrors were worth. It was probably better he should be doing that than trying to be a lawman.

I started to walk toward the kitchen, stopped, and pulled out my right-hand gun. Gawd, I was nervous as a chicken in a den of foxes. Why was I holding a gun just to walk around a house that didn't seem to have nobody in it? I slid it back in the holster.

I stopped in front of the kitchen door and put my ear to the panel. I heard voices but couldn't make out what they were saying. Then I realized by the soft tone it was women speaking Mexican. I wrapped my fingers around the butt of my right-hand gun and slowly opened the door with my left. Luisa and Francisca were sitting at the big kitchen table cutting some kind of vegetables into wooden bowls. At first they didn't hear me, and when I came to where they caught first sight, they both gave little yelps before they realized who it was.

"Mr. Jory," said Luisa in that soft Mexican tone that always makes me feel like whichever woman said it had romantic feelings toward me. I know that sounds crazy but there's something in the voices of these females when they talk American that makes me go all squishy. The men have a sharper tone that still sounds kind of nice, but it isn't the same. Even an old Mexican lady can seem just like a young girl when she goes into that purr.

"The *señora* is not in *casa*," said Luisa. "She and the *señor* have gone off on their horses very early. She told me they will not be eating again until tonight."

Eating? Just hearing her say the word was enough to make my stomach rumble and to look over at the stove, where two pots were bubbling away. Luisa caught my look; she knew me from the days before.

"Have you eaten, Señor Jory?" she asked. "We could make you something quickly."

"I have two others with me," I said.

"That is of no matter," she answered. "We have so much that we can feed even you and have some left over for others."

She and Francisca thought that was so funny that they held their sides and laughed within themselves. I can never get over how Mexican women always laugh without making any noise. I've seen some in saloons that sound like a calf braying, but the home ones, the nice ones, always keep it bottled up like it was something they didn't want to pour out before they had to.

I sat down at the table while Luisa took a plate and went over to the stove, and Francisca brought out another big wooden bowl and started shaping tortillas. It took a few minutes and I could feel my mouth gathering water, and I had to gulp a few times to keep from drowning right there and then.

I dug in with the spoon as soon as they put the plates on the table, and good as Mrs. Davis' cooking was, there wasn't nothing better than what I was shoveling down. The beans had some kind of meat in them that fell apart as soon as you bit into it, and there was a sweetness to the whole thing that wasn't like they had poured sugar in it but came from a mix of some kind of vegetables or the fat from the meat.

I was halfway through the plate when I remembered Guthrie and Andy out there, who had to be as hungry as I was. Well, maybe not as hungry, but hungry enough. So I got up and went out to the hall, where Guthrie was sitting in one of the big chairs with his head hanging down. I thought he might be sleeping, but as soon as he heard my boots on the wood floor, he looked right up.

"There's some grub in the kitchen," I told him, "and it's as good as you'd find anywhere."

"I'm not hungry," he said.

"It's nigh on midday," I told him, "and you've got to put something in your belly."

"I don't want nothing to eat," he said.

He looked kind of pale and sick, and I wondered if he'd suddenly come down with something. After all, he was a very old man and things can happen to them out of a clear blue sky. I wondered what it was like to be old and get tired easy and maybe sick all the time. Nobody had seemed stronger or hardier than Mr. Barron, but Roy had said that his face just turned all red and he had keeled over. That was probably because he was old. He had to have been near fifty, the same as Guthrie. Well, I wasn't going to push him if he didn't feel hungry.

I went back to the kitchen and asked Francisca if she would fill up a plate for my friend outside, and she gave me a big one with tortillas and beans and a spoon to go with it. I carried it real careful to the outside and stood on the porch and looked up the hill at the clump of trees, where I couldn't see anything, but I knew Andy had to be in there somewhere because that's where I had told her to be and that's what she would do. I almost yelled and waved for her to come down, but I didn't want to get Guthrie upset all over again, especially when he didn't look so good.

So I mounted up on Bones, which wasn't that easy with a full plate of hot beans in my hands, and rode up the hill to the clump. When I got into it, there was Andy standing by a rock with her rifle in her hand.

"I brought you some vittles," I told her.

She nodded and took the plate out of my hand. I hadn't spilled one bean.

"You got your water bottle with you?" I asked. She shook her head no. I took mine off the saddle and handed it to her.

"I've told you before how important water is," I told her. "I don't want you ever riding off again anywhere without a full water bottle."

She nodded again.

"You all right here?"

She nodded.

"I don't know how much longer we're going to be down there," I told her. "Crutchfield and Miss Amy rode off somewhere early and the kitchen ladies don't know when they'll be back. So you just set here and take it easy, but keep a watch as best you can who might be coming in. If it's the whole gang of them, we might want to get out and rethink the situation."

She nodded and I turned the horse and left her standing there with the beans in one hand, the water bottle in the other and her rifle tight between her legs. I wondered if she slept with her guns in her bed. She took them inside the privy with her, and sleeping was the only other thing I hadn't seen her do.

I rode back down and got off the horse. We had watered them at the hole on the other side of the hill before we had come down, but I didn't like them standing in the hot sun like that, so I brought them under the one tree standing to the left of the house and looped their reins over a branch. Bones turned his head and gave me a kiss on the ear. Damn crazy horse.

Guthrie was still sitting where I had left him, but this time he didn't even lift his head, so I just went past him into the kitchen. My heart sank when I saw my plate was gone from the table, but within a minute Luisa had brought me a full hot one from the stove. I ate until I could feel my belly pushing against my gun belt and then waved my hand at Luisa when she looked to see if I wanted more.

"It is good to eat your cooking once more," I told her, and she gave me a big smile. It's strange how I start to talk funny when I speak to Mexicans in American. It's like I'm speaking to a judge or someone important, and even my voice sounds different to me. I wished I knew more Mexican so I could talk to these people in their own language, which would be the polite thing to do, but I just knew the few words I'd picked up from the Mexican hands when I'd worked on the ranch before, and a lot of those were swear words. I'd also picked up a few words from Conchita, but I wasn't sure what they were and I was afraid to use them in polite company. I wondered whether she was still on the ranch, but I thought it would be embarrassing to ask Luisa or Francisca, so I just let it go.

Guthrie had taken off his hat and I could see the sweat shining on his face even though the room was cool because of the thick walls. He had to be coming down with something, and I wondered if we should be getting him back to town, where the barber could look him over to see what ailed him. But we had to finish this up some time, and he was more likely to get sicker than better at his age, so I didn't say anything.

As a matter of fact, I was thinking more about going into the big room and sinking into one of the padded chairs for a little bit, but I was worried I might get too comfortable and with all those beans in me maybe fall asleep. But while I was debating the matter with myself, the choice was made for me because there was a clatter of hooves outside in the front and that meant we were getting company. There couldn't have been a whole troop of them because Andy hadn't fired no shot but it sounded like more than one.

I went to the side window and looked out and there were four of them getting down, Miss Amy and Crutchfield and two of the white punchers. The rest of the men could be at the bunkhouse or the barn or the corral, but that was something we would have to find out later.

Guthrie put his hat back on his head but didn't move from the chair.

"Come on, old man," I said. "We've got business to do."

It came to me as I started to open the door that I hadn't ought to have called him old man. But that's what I had been thinking and that's how it had come out of my mouth. He didn't seem to notice none, but he did get out of his chair and walk over.

"Stay behind me and out of the way," I said as I pulled the door open and started out. Everything was backward from what it ought to of been. Here I was walking out of their house to meet them instead of them coming out to meet us. And it should have been the U.S. marshal leading the way instead of me. However, the whole thing was upside down, and I was just going to have to try to turn things right side up.

★ 19 ★

Miss Amy had already handed her reins to one of the punchers, so she was the first one to turn around and see us. She didn't say nothing, just stared like she was looking at a ghost. Crutchfield was talking to the other one about something, so I was partly down the stairs before he caught sight.

"What the hell is going on here?" he yelled, and I wondered if he used words like that in front of Miss Amy all the time. His face turned all red, and I kind of hoped he might keel over the way Mr. Barron had. That would sure have solved a lot of problems. Except he wasn't that old, so all a red face meant from him was that he was mad clear through. The two ranch hands didn't know what was going on, and they just stood there with both sets of reins in their hands, which meant they'd have to make two moves in order to get their guns out. Crutchfield didn't seem to be wearing a gun; at least I couldn't see one on him.

"Mr. Crutchfield," I said, "this is U.S. Marshal Tyrone Guthrie, and he has business with you." Guthrie was still somewhere behind me—probably on the porch because I hadn't heard no heels banging down the steps—but I wasn't going to turn to see exactly where he was because there were three of them in front of me and that's where I wanted to be looking. Miss Amy was standing in the line of fire between me and one of the punchers, and I wanted to tell her to move to the left a bit, but I didn't quite know how to say that because of the way things were.

"Miss Amy, would you move over there in case I have to shoot the man behind you?" That would have sounded real strange. It's amazing the things you do or don't do because they're not polite.

"What the hell kind of business has he got with me?" said Crutchfield, his voice still loud enough to call the hogs in from over the mountain. There he went using that word again.

I was waiting for Guthrie to tell him, or at least come down the steps to stand beside or in front of me, but there still wasn't any sound coming from the rear. Gawd, but I wanted to turn around and look, but pretty soon everybody would be sniffing the breeze and finding trouble there, and the second those two men dropped those reins I was going to have to move.

"He has a warrant to serve on you," I told him, "a warrant from the United States government itself. Marshal Guthrie, would you come down here and tell Mr. Crutchfield what this is all about?"

Finally, there was the sound of boots coming down the stairs, one at a time, real slow. I could feel the little man moving up beside me, and I hoped he wouldn't come too close to my right arm because I didn't want to have to move over and at the same time I didn't want to be crowded there. It's like when you're dealing with a rattlesnake: you're pretty safe if you don't stir, but the second it sees motion, it strikes. It was the same with those two cowhands. While we were talking, they would just be watching until they found out which way the wind was blowing. But the second Crutchfield yelled for them to do something, or I made a move that showed I had guns in mind, they would go into action. I didn't know how good they were, but everybody gets lucky once in a while, and nobody can be the death of you as quick as somebody.

"Are you Jasper L. Crutchfield?" Guthrie asked.

Gawdamighty. I suppose there are certain rules you

have to follow if you're a United States marshal, but that one seemed real silly. I had already called him Mr. Crutchfield, and anybody could tell that he was Miss Amy's husband and the boss man of this spread.

"What if I am?" said Crutchfield, his voice lower than it had been.

"I have here a warrant for your arrest," said Guthrie, pulling the paper out of his pocket and holding it out toward the big man.

I wondered just how big Crutchfield might be. I was one inch over six feet, but I felt small standing near to this man. His hands were big enough to cover a tortilla, and he looked almost as big as the horse he was standing next to.

Miss Amy made a noise, what kind I couldn't tell, but I still had my eyes on Crutchfield and the two punchers and couldn't look at her. I wondered how she felt about my coming out here to help arrest her husband. She said that she didn't like him no more and that she wanted to be shut of him, but I'd heard lots of wives talk that way about their husbands and then turn completely around when something happened. After all, a husband is a husband and a wife is a wife, and they swear on a bible to stick together, no matter what. What if Miss Amy had changed her mind since she'd last talked to me? I wished I was anyplace but where I was.

"What the hell do you mean you have a warrant for my arrest?" bellowed Crutchfield, looking like a bull that's got you against a fence. "On what grounds would you have a warrant for my arrest?" He looked at the two punchers, who were still holding the reins, and I could see that they were beginning to think about what the next move might be.

"The warrant states that while you were a captain in the United States Army, you did defraud the government of sums of money and took possession of cattle that were the property of the United States." Guthrie's voice was getting stronger as he went along. As a matter of fact, the old coot was beginning to sound like a United States marshal ought to.

"That's preposterous," said Crutchfield. That was the second time I had heard anybody use that word, and I stuck it in my brain as having a nice sound to it. "I never defrauded anybody of any money and I never took cattle that belonged to the government. Why would I do that? We've got thousands of cattle right here, more cattle than we know what to do with. There are any number of fellow officers who would vouch for my character and integrity. How do I know you're a United States marshal? How do I know who trumped up these charges against me?"

"I was appointed by President Ulysses S. Grant himself," said Guthrie, his voice sounding spunkier than I had yet heard it, "and the charges were made all legal like by lawyers from the United States Army and lawyers from the government of the United States. You can find out all about it when we get to Austin, but right now I'm telling you to stop all this palavering and come along as you're told."

Guthrie pulled the hand irons from the back of his belt and started walking toward Crutchfield. The iron bracelets looked like they weighed more than the marshal himself, but the thing that bothered me was that he was carrying them in his right hand. How was any man going to be able to pull a gun hanging on his right side if his fingers was busy doing other work?

Funny, I thought for a second we might get away with it, but talking about it is one thing and doing it is quite another. We were all watching Guthrie advancing on Crutchfield, and I guess we weren't thinking about anything else because the marshal couldn't have stood up much higher than the big man's belt, and the whole thing seemed so crazy that you wanted to see how it come out once he reached him.

"There's no way I'm going with you," yelled Crutchfield, "so stay away from me."

But the little man kept right on going toward him,

holding those hand irons in front of him, and by the time he reached the big fellow I was convinced that he was going to snap those on and we would be on our way just like that. Sometimes I'm so dumb that it's a wonder I get my boots on the proper legs.

Just as Guthrie was shoving forward the irons as though he expected Crutchfield to put his hands to meet him halfway, the big man reached down and grabbed the marshal around the waist, twisted him front to back, and lifted him up in front of him. Once he got him there, he pulled the marshal's gun out of his holster and stuck it straight out at me. At the same time he yelled to the two punchers to "Shoot! Shoot!"

The one on the right of me did drop the reins and go for his gun, but I drilled him in the shoulder before the piece was out of his holster and he went down on the ground, yelling and flapping his body all over the place. He had done pretty good considering that he had to make two motions, but it wasn't good enough. As I swung my gun to cover the other one, I had to stop because Miss Amy was still in the way, and I might have been dead except that the second puncher was still standing there holding the reins of the horses. When he saw what I was doing, he did make a move. He dropped the lines of the horses he was holding and put both hands up in the air. He didn't want any part of what was happening.

But just as I was thanking my lucky stars for small favors, a bullet ripped by my ear close enough for me to feel the breeze. I threw myself to the right to get away from Miss Amy and came up from the roll ready to shoot back, but Crutchfield was holding the marshal in such a way that there wasn't no chance to get at him.

"Drop your gun," Crutchfield yelled at me, "or I kill both you and this little bugger right off."

I suppose it would have been funny if we weren't going to have what there was of our brains blowed away. Crutchfield was holding the marshal in front of him like he was a big rag doll, and there wasn't no way I could get at him without maybe putting a bullet into the wrong body. If I dropped the gun I had out, I would still have the one in my left holster, and he might think I couldn't pull it fast enough to get him or he might just forget it was there. All I needed was for him to put the marshal down or maybe just move him to the side a bit, and I would have a chance with the left-hand gun. I was thinking positive about this because Crutchfield had missed me with the marshal's gun and we weren't that far away from each other. Sure, the bullet had whizzed close to my ear, but it ought to have gone right through my head if he was any kind of a shooter.

"Barnes," Crutchfield yelled, "you ride out and tell Stark to come back here with all the men."

"I don't want no part of this, Mr. Crutchfield," Barnes said. "That's a U.S. marshal you're hugging, and that's deeper water than I want to swim in."

"You do what I tell you," said Crutchfield, "or you're fired."

"That saves me from quitting," said the man. "I'm going to pick up my stuff at the bunkhouse and be out of here right smart. I don't want nothing that has to do with a U.S. marshal."

He dropped the reins of Miss Amy's horse, jumped up to his saddle and was out of there. The one who was shot had stopped thrashing about but was still laying there whimpering.

"Amy," Crutchfield said, "you ride out and get Stark. They can't be that far away by now."

"What did you steal?" she asked. "Why does the United States government want to put you in jail?"

"It's all a mistake," said Crutchfield. "Somebody made a mistake. I can clear it up. You go get Stark."

"If you can clear it up," she said, "then why don't you just go along with the marshal and the sheriff? I don't know why you're acting like this if you're an innocent man."

"You just do what you're told," he yelled, "or I'll kill your sweetheart here, and maybe you too."

Did you ever hear such crazy talk as that? The man had just said that he was going to kill his own wife. I doubt that anybody else in the whole world had ever said anything like that, or ever would. I was so mad that I thought for a second of pulling the trigger and devil take the hindmost. If I put the bullet in the right spot, it would go right through Guthrie and hit Crutchfield hard enough to make him let go or maybe even fall down. But I couldn't gun down the little man no matter how bad he was at his job. And even then, the bullet might not go all the way through and hit Crutchfield. My best bet was to lay down the gun in my hand and hope to get a chance to pull with the left.

"You put that gun down, Sheriff," said Crutchfield, shifting his full attention back on me, "or I'm going to shoot right now."

I bent over and laid the gun on the dirt. There was no way I would ever drop a gun and maybe ruin it. Crutchfield kept moving toward me, but he always had the marshal in such a way that pulling my left-hand gun would have done no better than it would have been with the right one. He came up so close to me that if he'd pushed out his hand, he could have put the barrel right on my nose, and as we stood there face to face, I could see that look in his face and feel the pull as his finger tightened on the trigger, and I knew he was going to shoot me right in the head and then maybe finish off the marshal.

I was just about to throw myself sideways in hopes of making him miss, but at that distance he would have got me no matter how far I jumped. It made me mad that I was going to be killed by a man like this, who really wasn't that good with a gun and who would still be husband to Miss Amy. I knew I only had a second and I decided to butt ahead into him instead of jumping away, even though there was barely no chance, and the marshal was hanging there like a dead man without the least idea of kicking or twisting to help me out.

But just as I went into it, a bullet whined down out of nowhere and Crutchfield fell to the ground, dropping his gun just as it went off and dropping the marshal along with it. Crutchfield was grabbing his right leg with both hands and yelling bloody murder as red poured out between his fingers. I don't know where the bullet from his gun had gone, and at first I thought that maybe he had shot himself, but that couldn't have been. There were two shots.

And then it hit me. Up there on the hill on the edge of those trees was Deputy Sheriff Andy Colvin, and once again she had saved my life from being killed. Gawdamighty but that was some shot, even with a rifle at that distance. She had plugged that big man in the only spot that was showing to her and it couldn't have been showing too much. I never could have done it in a million years, and I doubt that there was any man in the whole world who could have matched it.

I picked the marshal up and tried to set him on his feet, but his body wasn't having none of that. He wobbled around like you see the drunks do in saloons sometimes, and everybody laughs at them. But this wasn't funny at all. Part of his problem it turned out was that Crutchfield had squeezed him so tight that he'd cut off his air and it took him a minute to get breathing again. As soon as he could, he reached down with the irons to where Crutchfield was holding his two hands together around his wound, which made it easy to snap them around the bloody wrists.

Miss Amy ran over to her husband, undid his neckerchief, lifted his hands off the leg, and tied the piece of cloth around the bullet hole as hard as she could. That made my heart sink as I watched her do it. But then she turned around and did the same thing for the puncher as best she could. He wasn't nothing to her, so what she was doing was being a nice lady. At least that's what I wanted to believe.

"Sheriff," Andy yelled from above, "you want me to come down there?"

"No," I yelled back. "You stay right where you are and keep watch to see if Stark's coming with the rest of the hands. We've got to get out of here as fast as we can."

I turned to the marshal and said, "I don't think either of these two can ride a horse to town, but we'll have to do the best we can with that."

"You can have one of the wagons," said Miss Amy, and she went running off to the barn.

I walked over to the one with the wound in his shoulder and asked him how he was doing.

"You nigh killed me," he said. "I can't go nowhere."

"You tried to shoot the sheriff of Barron County," I told him, "and maybe even a United States marshal. You're going to jail."

It didn't take maybe ten minutes before Miss Amy came riding up with a buggy big enough for four, and two horses that looked like they could run like the wind for as long as you needed. She couldn't have hitched them up so fast without some help, but there weren't no Mexicans with her. They probably wanted no part of this whole thing.

"Sheriff, I can see dust to the south," Andy yelled down from the hill.

"You come on down here," I told her. "We've got to go back on the wagon track."

By the time she came down I had both Crutchfield and the puncher in the back of the buggy and had hitched Bones to the back.

"Can you ride all right?" I asked Guthrie, "or do you want to drive the wagon?"

"I'll ride," he said, and mounted up on his horse. He did it slow but he looked like he could go the distance we needed.

I jumped up on the seat and gave the horses a crack with the reins. They started off at a pretty pace, and I figured we just might have enough of a lead to get to town before anybody could catch up with us. It wasn't until we were almost out of the yard that I remembered and turned to look at Miss Amy. She was standing there all alone with blood red on her white shirt, looking at us in a strange way. It was too far by then to tell if she was crying, but I had a feeling she was, and I wondered who it might be for.

Just before we turned the corner I saw both Luisa and Francisca run out of the house and grab her on each side. I felt better that they would be taking care of her. But I wondered again who she might be crying for, and I gave the horses a big slap on the rump with the reins and yelled like a Comanche.

I suddenly remembered that I hadn't said nothing to Andy about saving my skin again. I looked over at her galloping alongside, but she was staring straight ahead, and as usual the look on her face wasn't no different than it ever was.

★ 20 ★

As soon as we rode up to the jail, I sent Andy to find the barber so he could do something about the hurts of Crutchfield and his hired man. The barber was so excited that his hands were shaking, and he could barely wait to get out of there to spread the news. He kept apologizing to Crutchfield whenever he had to pull or push something and especially when he poured the whiskey over the two holes in the flesh, but Crutchfield didn't say a word. It was like he had turned into a block of stone. With his size, it was more like a mountain of stone.

Somebody had to have noticed that there was a U.S. marshal in town, and they probably started putting two and four together when we came in hauling two men in the back of a buggy. You know how people are; they probably started thinking up all kinds of stories that had nothing to do with what was really going on.

The barred part of the jail wasn't barely big enough to hold four prisoners, and I was in a fix about that until Andy came up with the answer.

"Why don't we send these two back to the ranch in the buggy?" she asked me, pointing at the ones we had been feeding and watering and getting fertilized by in the past week.

"And why don't we send the new one with them and just keep Crutchfield?" I answered, which is what we did.

One of the first two prisoners said he could drive all right. I guess he and his partner were so glad to be shut of jail that they would have taken the offer if they had to hold the reins in their teeth. By the time they went off, there was already a little crowd across the street gawking at us as we went in and out. They all watched while we loaded the three men into the buggy, buzzing away to each other and standing there even after the dust trail had blown away. It's true that there isn't much to do in a town our size, but you'd think they had some kind of business to attend to rather than just spending the day staring at a beat-up old building.

Since the barber was in charge of spreading the news, it didn't take long for the word to get to every nook and cranny of the place. Inside of half an hour I had a visit from the town fathers, who wanted to know what in tarnation was going on. As usual, Tom Kraft did most of the talking.

"What have you done?" he asked, and for a second I thought he was going to wring his hands together, but what he was really doing was trying to wipe the sweat off his palms. "You have wounded and arrested and thrown into jail the head of the biggest ranch in the area. Do you know how much money the Barron people bring into town each week? Each day? This is crazy. Plain crazy. How do you explain all this?"

Since the jail was hardly bigger than a barrel, all this talk was going on right in front of Crutchfield, who was leaning against the back wall of the barred part with blankets under and in back of him. He still didn't say nothing, just kept staring at me like a hawk circling a field full of baby rabbits. The wound in his leg wasn't a very bad one, because Andy had shot through the fleshy part and the bullet had gone right through. He just sat there and watched and listened as Kraft and Brecht and Jenkins argued his case.

At one point, Kraft turned to Crutchfield and said, "I know this is all a big mistake, Mr. Crutchfield, one that will be cleared up as soon as possible. Meanwhile, if there is anything I can do to make your stay easier or more comfortable, you just speak up and it will be done. Do you want more blankets or some pillows? Is there anything special you want to eat? Just say the word. All you have to do is say the word.''

Then Kraft turned to me and asked if maybe Crutchfield couldn't be kept in a more comfortable place until the matter was straightened out.

''Look,'' I told them, ''this whole thing has nothing to do with me or the town. That man over there is a United States marshal and he has a warrant for Mr. Crutchfield's arrest, and if you have any questions, then you ask him to give you the answers.''

They all turned on Guthrie, who was sitting on a chair staring at Crutchfield the way he had stared at that prisoner the first time I had met him. The old bird looked tired, his face more gray than brown. He'd been flying pretty hard since morning, what with the rides both ways and being clutched to Crutchfield's chest like he was a good-looking dance-hall girl, and then having his gun taken away like he was a baby. One of my pa's favorite words was ''humiliating.'' He always thought somebody was trying to ''humiliate'' him, and when I look back on it, I guess they were. Well, it's hard to think of anything more humiliating than having your gun taken away from you. A little bit of a shiver went through me when I thought back on Crutchfield making me lay my gun down in the dirt. But no one had ever, and no one was ever going to, yank my gun out of my holster and get the drop on anybody. Whenever I watched a horse being gelded, I gave a little shiver because they had taken something away from him that would change him for the rest of his born days. That's what the marshal looked like. I suppose there isn't much difference from being an old coot and being gelded, but it's still not the same thing. The marshal wasn't a gunslinger, that was for sure, but he was still a lawman, and still a man, and he had to be squatting there thinking dark thoughts about the past and maybe the future.

He also had to have been thinking about how he was

going to get Crutchfield to Austin, and I figured I would get that straightened out with him right after the council yapped itself out. There wasn't no question in my mind that he wouldn't be able to do it on horses because it would be mighty difficult for a wounded man to ride all that distance. It also would be nigh on impossible for the marshal to bulldog any sized man and hold him tight just to get him across the street, let alone to Austin.

No, the best way would be to take him by stage, which would be coming through the next day. Crutchfield would be in irons, and there would be the driver and whoever was riding shotgun. I could tell them to make sure that Crutchfield was not sitting near enough to grab the marshal's gun again, nor that of anybody else on the stage. It would be like when Mrs. Davis had one of the neighborhood girls over to watch Todd when she had to go somewhere at night. One of those girls, Tessie Plunkett, would have more chance of getting Crutchfield to Austin than the marshal would.

Kraft was asking Guthrie what the charges were, and he told them it had something to do with stealing money and cattle from the United States Army and that was all he knew about it.

"You want to know more," he told them, "you ask the lawyer people from the government. I'm just a marshal doing my sworn duty."

They didn't seem to have no more questions about why Crutchfield had been arrested and put in jail. Have you ever noticed that wherever the United States government is concerned, everybody shuts up? They might tell a town marshal or a sheriff or a council member to stick his head in a privy, but once the words "United States" are mentioned, people figure it's bigger than anything they can handle and they let it happen or walk away. I sure hoped the federal government stayed right about everything they did.

"Well," said Kraft, "I guess we'll have to wait and see how this comes out. I'm sure there's been a mistake about

Mr. Crutchfield stealing anything, but the responsibility lays with the marshal and the sheriff, and the town council has nothing to do with the matter.''

My pa told me once about how a Roman named Pontius Pilate washed his hands after he sentenced Jesus to be crucified and that was supposed to take all the blame off him. My pa said you didn't need any soap and water, that most people did it with words. That's what the town council was doing with Crutchfield. They let him know that they didn't think he was guilty of anything in case he got off and came back to run the Barron ranch again, and then they told the marshal and me that we were the ones who were doing all this and it would be on our heads if it did go wrong. I didn't care. I was like everybody else. I figured the United States government wouldn't have brought the charges if he wasn't guilty of them.

After the councilmen left, I talked to Guthrie about how he was going to get Crutchfield to Austin. He started to tell me that he came by horse and by God he was going back by horse, but it had taken him nine days to get to Barronsville and there weren't that many towns in between if you wanted to bed down somewhere for the night instead of living on the trail.

I told him that the stage would be going through the next afternoon, and he could put his prisoner inside of it and tie his horse to the back of it and get to Austin without worrying none about going by the trail. He said he didn't have enough money to pay for all that, and I told him that the stage people and everybody else would trust the United States government to pay for it later. I didn't know whether this was true or not, but I wanted both him and Crutchfield to make it to Austin, and even though what I said might have been close to a lie to some people, including me, it could also end up true.

''You just show your badge and papers to anybody who asks,'' I told him, ''and they'll give you whatever you need.''

I asked the marshal where he planned to stay that night,

and he said he was going to stay right there with his prisoner. So I sent Andy out to get food for the two of them and said she should get her own eats while she was at it. When she came back, I told her I was going to the Davis house to have my own supper and then I would be back.

"If the marshal's going to stay here with the prisoner all night," I said, "then I'm going to stay along with him." You know something? It made me feel real good to keep calling Crutchfield "the prisoner." I kept thinking of him and Miss Amy being in bed together and how he had probably hit her in the face and how he was boss of the whole Barron ranch, that could have been mine if I had wanted it, and it made me both mad and sad. I don't know at who or why, but it was there burning inside of me. What made it even worse was that I was so hungry when Andy brought the two tins of food and the coffee that I almost took a slice of bread off Crutchfield's plate before she gave it to him. I would have gotten him another one, but that didn't make me feel any better about what I almost did.

So I stayed for a while longer on purpose just to punish myself for being so greedy. I'd been hungry on the trail plenty of times before, so it wasn't like it was no new thing happening to me. Maybe I still wasn't as growed up as I should be.

"I'm going back to Mrs. Davis' for my vittles," I told Andy, "and then I'll circle the town and then I'll come back here and you can go home to sleep."

"I'm staying here tonight," she said.

"There's no need for you to stay," I told her. "I'll keep the marshal company. Besides, there ain't room enough for all three of us to stretch out."

"Then I'll stand up," she said.

"Look," I told her, "there's no reason why there has to be three lawmen to guard just one prisoner. You'll go on home like I told you."

"It's best I stay here," she said.

"Why?"

"Well," she said, "supposing those people ride in from the ranch to get their boss out?"

Gawdamighty! That girl should have been sheriff instead of me. That Stark had enough men out there to shoot this whole town away if they had a mind to, and there was no reason to think that they might not have a mind to. There was nobody in town to fight off a bunch like that except for us, and you couldn't count on the marshal for any big help no matter what happened. I wished that stage was there and the two of them was on their way, but that was just wishing. The big question was whether I should even go out to eat my supper or to stay there in case anything happened. My stomach answered that one for me.

"I'll go eat fast," I said, "and do the town real quick and be back here as soon as a horse can switch his tail. You keep this door barred, and if there's any trouble, just shoot your gun through the roof and I'll come a-running."

Andy nodded. She had already used up so many words that she probably felt faint. The marshal didn't say nothing, just sat there staring at his prisoner.

I waited outside until I heard Andy bar the door, and then I went quick to Mrs. Davis' house, where she had some food staying hot on the back of the stove.

"How's everything going?" she asked, looking as neat and trim as a woman can be.

"Well," I said, "we've got Mr. Crutchfield in the jail and—"

"I've heard all about that," she said. "I was just wondering if you're expecting any trouble from the Barron hands."

There it was again. Two women had thought of something that I had ought to have thought of by myself. I was beginning to wonder if maybe I wasn't smart enough to be a sheriff. It's one thing to be able to use a gun but quite another to think ahead and outsmart whoever might give you trouble. I had a sad feeling that Mrs. Davis' husband would have thought ahead like that if he was still sheriff. And alive. He might have been smart, but he figured wrong when he went down that alley that night. Well, at least I had my guns if I didn't have the brains.

"I'm going to stay over at the jail tonight," I told Mrs. Davis, "and I'd like to take my blankets if it's all right with you."

"You going to be there alone?" she asked.

"Nope. The marshal and Andy are going to be there, too."

I said it like I had thought ahead to what the Barron people might do, and had then decided that this was the right thing.

"That girl's going to be there with you men all night?" she asked, and her voice sounded so different that I looked at her quick.

"That deputy's going to be there," I told her.

She didn't say anything more, so I took the blankets and walked around town with them under my arm, looking through the doors of the saloons rather than going in. It was one of those real quiet nights when everybody seemed to go home to bed early, and there weren't many strangers drifting through. I got back to the jail and knocked on the door.

"Who's there?" Andy asked.

I'd have bet my pay that she had that rifle or shotgun trained dead center from the opposite side. "It's Jory."

She unbolted the door, let me in, then bolted it up again. She had the rifle in her hand. That can go through wood better than a shotgun shell no matter what you had it stuffed with.

The marshal was still sitting there staring at his prisoner. He hadn't eaten but half of what Andy had brought him, and when I looked into the barred section, I saw that Crutchfield hadn't eat none of his. His being so quiet was beginning to get on my nerves. I wondered what was going on in his mind. Maybe he was thinking of what it was going to be like to go to jail, or maybe he was thinking about how he might bust out of there, or maybe he was thinking that maybe Stark and his boys were going to show up and get him out.

"We can take turns staying awake," I said. "Andy, why don't you lay down on these blankets in the corner and get the first snooze?"

"I'm not sleepy," she said, sliding down the wall until her rump hit the floor. "I'll just sit here."

"You want to get some rest?" I asked Guthrie. He was beginning to shrivel up more and more each time I looked at him.

"I'm fine," he said.

"Well," I said, "I think I'll just sit down by this wall the way Andy's doing over there."

So I did it, thinking that I'd listen real hard and watch close when the girl and the old man dropped off. I must have fallen asleep right away because it was the roosters crowing that cut through the dream I was having and brought me back to sheriffing.

at me. just kept his eyes on the ma

★ 21 ★

I had drunk four cups of coffee with my dinner because somebody had once told me that there's something in coffee that helps you keep awake. Since I had slept sounder than Todd Davis the whole night through, I found out that my leg had been pulled once again. Sometimes people tell you the biggest lies with such a serious face that it's like it's coming straight from heaven.

What that coffee did do when I woke up was make me want to turn a dry bed into a raging river. When I climbed to my feet, Andy did the same from the opposite wall, and it made me wonder if maybe she was having the same problem I was. Ladies first.

"Andy," I said, "why don't you go out and do what you have to?"

"I don't have to do nothing," she said.

I wondered whether she'd slept at all during the night. The marshal looked like he'd been awake the whole time, his eyes still staring in at Crutchfield, who was staring right back at him. It's too bad the marshal wasn't as good at marshaling as he was at staring.

"You might see about getting us some breakfast in here," I said, "and some water and maybe get the barber to look at the prisoner's leg again."

If she had those chores to do, then she could take care of whatever else she needed and nobody would be the wiser. As soon as she left, I asked Crutchfield if maybe he wanted to use one of the buckets, but he didn't even look at me, just kept his eyes on the marshal. I wondered if maybe I shouldn't go along to Austin with them, but that would have left the town without a sheriff and they weren't paying me to go traipsing off on federal-government business.

"Sheriff," somebody yelled from outside. It was the kind of yell that made you know right then that something was wrong.

"Sheriff," the man called again. "You come on out, Sheriff."

"Who's there?" I shouted back through the door. "What do you want?"

"We want you, Sheriff. We've come to take Mr. Crutchfield back to the ranch where he belongs, and if you don't bring him out, we're going to shoot down the building."

"You shoot down the building," I said, "and you're going to have one dead Crutchfield along with everybody else."

I looked quick around the room. We didn't have no windows. During the daytime, we kept the door open for light, and at night we used the lantern. The walls were barely thick enough to stop a fair-sized rock, but bullets would come through like croton oil through a short man. We could lay down flat on the floor, but if they were shooting from horses, the bullets would angle down right at us. The voice. It had to be Stark's voice. I wondered how many men he had with him.

"Then you better bring him on out," Stark said, "and maybe nobody will get hurt."

The marshal stood up and pulled his gun from the holster. It took a while. He turned to face the door. "You fire one shot in here," he said, "and the first one who will be hit will be the prisoner. No matter where the shot goes, the prisoner dies from it."

That was quick thinking. Nobody could ever prove what shot it was that killed Crutchfield, whether it was fired from outside or from the marshal's gun. I wondered if the marshal had it in him to shoot down a prisoner in cold blood. Crutchfield was probably wondering the same thing because he yelled out, "Stark! Use your head. Don't do anything crazy."

"Don't worry, Mr. Crutchfield," Stark called out. "We're going to get you free nice and easy."

I remembered what that puncher had said out at the ranch when we had picked up Crutchfield. He didn't want no trouble with the federal government and he had skedaddled.

"You better not mess with the law, Stark," I said. "You've got a U.S. marshal in here and a sheriff. Anything happens to us and you're hunted men for the rest of your lives."

"Ain't nothing going to happen to you if you just bring out Mr. Crutchfield," Stark said. "He ain't done nothing and you got no right to keep him in there. His wife wants him back on the ranch."

"Is Miss Amy out there?" I asked.

"No, she ain't right now. But if we don't bring him home, she said she's going to come in and get him herself. But we do have a woman out here right now."

"What are you talking about?"

"We got someone who goes parading around like a man. But we don't think so, and if you don't come out here pronto, we're going to find out one at a time whether she's really a woman or not."

My knees were shaking and I felt I had to sit down before I fell down. They had Andy. They had Andy out there and she was the one who had made them crawl in the saloon that night. I thought of all those men going at Andy.

"We might have to find out twice," said Stark, and from the hoots of laughter I could tell that he had a real big crew with him.

I couldn't let them do anything to that girl. She'd fight them tooth and nail, but without her guns she was just a woman with a woman's strength, and they'd do her in so

that even if she lived, she'd never be alive anymore. Why
had I made her deputy? Everybody said it was crazy and
everybody was right. But how did I know they really had
her? How did I know if he was telling me true? She
answered that one herself.

"Don't do nothing, Sheriff," she yelled. "Don't give
up the prisoner."

Even through the door I heard the crack that only comes
when somebody's face has been slapped as hard as a man is
able. There wasn't no yell from her, no crying, no sound.
Either they had knocked her out, or it was just Andy being
herself. Nothing they could do would make that girl be
like a woman. But they had said they were going to find
out if she really was a woman, and on this thing I knew
that Stark was as good as his word.

"We're coming out," I shouted through the door.

"No, we ain't," Guthrie said to me. "A U.S. marshal
don't give up his prisoner."

"You do what you want, old man," I told him, "but I
ain't letting that girl go through anything because I didn't
do my job right. You can stay here if you want to, but I'm
going out there."

"Turn me loose," said Crutchfield. "That's all they
want. You send me out there and we'll all go back to the
ranch without any trouble. All you have to do is turn me
loose."

I could just see him keeping his word. Once he got out
there they would send enough bullets through the walls to
turn the place into sawdust.

"You can go out there if you want," said the marshal,
"but there ain't no way I am going to turn this prisoner
loose until I deliver him in Austin, alive or dead." He
turned to face Crutchfield again, his gun pointing right at
him. Guthrie was right. He had his sworn duty to do. But
a sheriff also has a responsibility to his deputy, and I
wasn't going to shirk from that. There was that word
"responsibility" again. That was the one Mr. Barron had
used when he talked to me about marrying up with Miss

Amy, and that was the one that had made me run off. But I realized now that you couldn't always run or hide where responsibility was concerned. If you were going to live in the world, then there came a time when you had to face it.

I unbarred the door and opened it a crack to let my eyes get accustomed to the light. Then I opened it only a little more and stepped out. I didn't want them seeing what was going on with the marshal and Crutchfield. It might keep them wondering enough to stay their hands.

There were eleven of them sitting on their horses and Stark on the ground standing ahead of his palomino. They all had handguns or rifles pointing at me except for Stark, whose gun was still in his holster. Laying at his feet was Andy, her skinny body all twisted in the dirt. I couldn't tell if she was dead or alive.

"You bring out Mr. Crutchfield," said Stark, "and we'll be on our way."

"Marshal says he isn't going to give him up. He says he'll kill him first."

"I guess we'll have to take our chances on that," said Stark. "You're going to be the first to die and then the marshal and then we're going to use the girl for a bit and then we're going to ride off with Crutchfield or without him. But if you turn him over to us now, we'll just say thank you and be on our way."

I looked down at Andy again. She had to be alive if he was talking like that. But I figured I was going to be dead along with the marshal no matter which way I turned.

"Stark," I said, "there ain't nobody in the world faster with a handgun than me. Every one of the men whose gun is pointing at me right now could shoot all at once, but before I hit the ground you would be dead."

"Let's give it a try," somebody said, and they all laughed.

Stark's face changed a bit and he held up his hand. "Whoa there a minute," he said. "We're all law-abiding citizens here. All we want is to get our boss, who has been unrightly charged with some fool thing. I served in the army with Captain Crutchfield, and I know him to be an honest, decent man.''

So there it was. "Parties unknown." Stark had to be one of those parties unknown who had robbed the government along with Crutchfield. If we let him loose, they would go back to the ranch, take whatever they wanted, round up a big herd of cattle and drive it off where they could sell it and make enough money to live the rest of their lives. I saw it all. But seeing it didn't help me in doing something about it.

"Look, Sheriff," said Stark, "you're all alone and there are twelve of us. All I have to do is lift my arm and your body is going to be holding enough bullets to start a lead mine. I don't think you can get a shot off, no matter how good you are. I doubt that old man in there can shoot the captain even if he holds the gun to his head. You're all alone.''

"No, he ain't," said a voice from my right, and I turned to see Roy limping up with a shotgun in his hand pointed straight at Stark.

"Jory," I heard a woman call to the left of me, and there was Mrs. Davis in her nightclothes, holding Todd in one hand and a rifle in the other, which she pointed in the general direction of all the men on the horses. Gawdamighty!

I was just about to yell at her to go on home when right behind her came Mr. Kraft and Lawyer Kane, both of them holding shotguns that they were pointing at the bunch in front of me. And then came Mr. Jenkins, and he was carrying one of them old buffalo guns that could blow a hole through a mountain. Behind him was a woman all dressed up fancy and with the damnedest little gold-plated gun in her hand that I ever did see. It was the dance-hall girl whose dress had been ripped down by Stark, and she pointed her little piece right at him. I doubt she could have hit him if she had stuck that thing in his ear, but she sure attracted attention with it. She must have been up all night to be still wearing her work clothes. I felt my throat go all lumpy and I could feel tears welling up in my eyes. If

somebody had told me these people would put their lives
on the line to save mine, I wouldn't have believed it for all
the tea in China. Except maybe for Roy. But there they
were. We were still outnumbered, but all those punchers
on the horses realized that some of them were going to die
if a shooting started, and you could tell by the way their
mounts shied around that they sensed that the men on top
were getting unrestful.

I don't know what would have happened then if the
sound of a stampede hadn't hit our ears like a thunderclap,
and we all looked to the right of me, where coming down
the road was a war party of some kind. They were raising
dust that seemed to go right to the sky, and I think I could
have gone around and lifted the guns of every one of those
Crutchfield people without them knowing it.

Gawdamighty, it was Miss Amy riding at the head of all
her Mexican hands, maybe twenty-five of them, and they
all held their rifles in their hands ready for business. Oh
my, I thought, she's come to help Stark and get her
husband out of jail. I knew this to be true when they
circled behind Stark's people to back them up if a showdown came.

Miss Amy rode to the front so that she was not two
paces from me. "What's going on here?" she asked.

"We're just trying to bring Captain Crutchfield home,"
said Stark.

"Why are you trying to do that?" she asked.

"Because he ain't done nothing, ma'am, and we were
trying to do right by him."

"Mr. Crutchfield has been charged with stealing by the
United States government," said Miss Amy. "I'm sure
he's innocent of these charges and will be cleared. But the
only way he can do that is if he goes to Austin and clears
himself. If you took him out of here now, he would be
running the rest of his life. He goes to Austin. Pedro."

It seemed like Iglesias was head wrangler again, because when she said that, all the Mexicans pointed their
rifles at Stark's men on the horses. The white punchers

didn't know what to do at first, but then one by one they put their handguns back in their holsters and their rifles into their saddle carriers. Mrs. Davis handed Todd over to the dance-hall girl and ran to where Andy was laying in the dirt.

"She's breathing," she said, "but we better get Mr. Dawkins here to look at her."

"Who hit her?" I called out to the bunch in front of me. Nobody answered. I walked over to where Stark was standing. "You're the one hit her," I said. I wasn't asking; I was telling.

I took hold of his arm and pulled him along with me to the edge of the whole bunch and then out to the middle of the street. A lot of people had come out of their houses, but when they saw us come out where they were, they ran to the sides. A town knows when something's going to happen.

"Stark," I said, "I'm going to back away about forty paces, and then I'm going to come back toward you. You've got your gun and nobody's going to step between us. You hit a deputy sheriff, and nobody does that in my town."

I turned to everybody over by the jailhouse and I said, "This is going to be a fair fight. If Stark comes through, I don't want you doing nothing to him. Let him ride out."

Then I started backing off down the middle of the street. I knew he wouldn't try anything because all those men were watching him, and if he pulled on my back, they would have gunned him down. But just the same, I backed away. Nobody takes care of yourself better than yourself. It wasn't fair what I was doing because he was one man against a whole town and they would never let him ride off if he killed me, but what he had done to Andy had made me mad clear through, maybe a little crazy, and I had to do something to him. Something. When I had backed off maybe forty paces, I called out, "All right, Stark. I'm coming for you," and I started the trip back.

This was the first time in my whole life that I wanted to

kill anybody just like that. There'd been more than enough times when I had gone against people and it was them or me, but what was in my mind now was different. He had hit my Andy, hit her so bad that maybe she was going to die. And he was going to pay for it.

As I took each step, I was waiting for him to make his move, trying in my mind to will him to pull so that I could go with both guns and see to it that he never hit nobody again in his life. But he just stood there facing me, standing with his shoulders hunched forward. The fingers of his right hand twitched once and I almost went for it, but he stopped dead and didn't do nothing.

I finally came right up to him, maybe one pace away, and I thought of faking a move to make him draw, but I could tell he wasn't going to do nothing. I don't know if it was me or the crowd that was all around, but he didn't have the belly for it.

I opened my right hand all the way and hit him on the side of the face as hard as I could, the palm smacking into him like it was a fist, and he almost went down to his knees, but he managed to hold himself up. Then I reached out my left hand and lifted his gun from the holster.

"You're under arrest," I told him. "You get back over by the jail building and wait." I turned my back to him and walked away.

"I want that man," the marshal yelled from the doorway. "I'm taking him to Austin to face charges of trying to free a federal prisoner. I want that man."

"What about the rest of them?" I asked.

"Can't handle them all," he said. "They belong to you."

I turned to Miss Amy. "You want them to work on your ranch anymore?"

She shook her head. "We'll take them back and let them get their stuff and then they are gone," she said.

"You people are getting off lucky," I told them. "But I want you to put all your guns on the ground, handguns and rifles. And if you're ever this way again, steer clear of

Barron County. I've put all your faces in my head, and if we ever meet again, you're going to pay double."

Not one of them made a move or said a word. Then they got off their horses and laid all their guns on the ground. Then they mounted up again.

"I'm going to be running the ranch again," said Miss Amy, soft enough so that only I could hear her. "This time I won't be afraid to do it."

"If your husband's cleared, he can come back," I said.

"We'll talk about that later," she said. "Come out to see me. There's a lot we've got to talk about."

Then she wheeled her horse, yelled something in Mexican, and her men herded those white punchers out of town like they was cattle. That was quite a girl, that Miss Amy. Quite a girl.

I turned again and there was Andy standing straight up, real pale but standing straight up.

"You doing all right?" I asked, even though half her face was swollen like she had twenty bee stings.

She nodded at me, picked up a rifle from the ground, walked over, grabbed Stark by the arm, and then led him into the jailhouse. All the townspeople started babbling and crowding around, and I thanked them one and all, those that had come with guns and those who had only come to watch.

"Mrs. Davis," I said, "I ain't never going to forget what you did this morning. That was one of the bravest things I ever seen. But why did you bring Todd along to a gunfight?"

"I don't know," she said. "I've just never left him alone, and there wasn't anybody to take care of him at this time of the morning. Are you going to be home for the noon meal?"

"I sure am," I told her. "I haven't had no breakfast."

Roy was still standing there and I went over and punched him on his good arm.

"I didn't think an old cripple could move as fast as you

did," I told him. "There's probably a foreman's job open at the Barron ranch, and I bet you could handle it."

"Those days are over," he said. "And besides, I have to stay in town to take care of you. Maybe you're the one should be out there running things. You said you were a foreman."

He said "things" in a funny way, and I knew he was talking about Miss Amy as well as the ranch.

"That's not a bad idea," I told him, "but I have to stay in town to take care of you."

★ 22 ★

The stagecoach was late, but it finally came roaring into town about the middle of the afternoon, and we loaded up Crutchfield, Stark, and the marshal. I talked to the driver and the guard, and they said they'd ride herd on them as best they could. We had dug out a pair of hand irons for Stark, too, and I felt better about that, although I wasn't sure just how much sand the man had in him when he didn't have a passel of people backing him up. They all had words for me before they got on the stage.

"I'll be back," said Crutchfield.

"I'll be waiting," I told him.

"I ain't going to forget this," said Stark.

"I like it when a man learns a lesson," I told him.

"Thank you for your assistance," said Marshal Guthrie. "I will put in my report how much help you were. And I'm going to send you a good chair and a desk for your office."

"Were you happy in the furniture business?" I asked him.

"Yes."

"You think about that," I told him.

And they were off.

Andy was tidying up the barred part of the room when I went back in. Her face was still all swole up, but I knew better than to tell her to take the rest of the day off. I wondered if she was learning as much about me as I was about her.

I sat down in the rickety chair. I would like to have leaned it against the wall, but I didn't want to get splinters up my rear. I wondered if Guthrie would really send a good chair and a desk. I'd like that.

"I'm going to buy a dress," Andy said. She was leaning on the broom looking at me.

"That's nice," I told her. "Mr. Kraft has some pretty ones hanging up." Lord, I thought to myself, I sure hope she ain't thinking of wearing a dress while she is deputying. People wouldn't go for that. Besides, I'd gotten used to her wearing a man's clothes. Wouldn't be Andy without them.

"My given name is Andrea," she said.

"That's a pretty name," I told her. I wished she hadn't of told me, though, because I liked thinking of her as Andy, and Andrea didn't seem right for a deputy sheriff.

"You thinking of getting married?" she asked.

"Now, why would I want to do that?" I wondered if that crack in the face had addled her brains a mite.

"A man reaches a certain age, he starts thinking about getting married," she said.

"I might someday," I told her, "but I got a few good years left in me yet."

"You can't marry Mrs. Crutchfield," said Andy, "because she's still married."

I just looked at her, figuring I better have the barber check her head again.

"And you can't marry Mrs. Davis," she said, "because she's too old."

"Well," I said, "I guess I ain't got nobody to marry."

"You got me," she said.

Here the girl never put more than two words together and now she was making a joke, a real funny joke. I started to laugh. I laughed so hard that I had to get off the chair and sit on the floor. Maybe it was because of what we had gone through that day, but I couldn't stop laughing. Tears were coming out of my eyes, and everything looked a little bit blurry, and I had to wipe them twice before they were clear enough for me to look at Andy again.

She wasn't laughing. Her face was as straight as when she was sighting her rifle. Then she started to laugh, too. Not as hard as I was, because laughing, like talking, didn't come natural to her. But I could tell she was trying. If she stuck with me for a while, I'd have her talking and laughing just like a regular woman does.

Gawd, I sure was a lucky man to have a deputy like this one.